Little Cabin
by the River

J o y c e   N e a l

3ABN
books

P.O. Box 220
West Frankfort, IL 62896

Pacific Press® Publishing Association
Nampa, Idaho
Oshawa, Ontario, Canada
www.pacificpress.com

Cover design by Pacific Press Publishing Association
Cover concept by Mary King
Cover illustration by Marcus Mashburn
Inside design by Aaron Troia
Editing by Bobby Davis

The author assumes full responsibility for the accuracy of all facts and quotations as cited in this book.

Additional copies of this book are available from two locations:
3ABN: Call 1-800-752-3226 or visit www.3ABN.org.
Adventist Book Centers: Call 1-800-765-6955 or visit http://www.adventistbook center.com.

3ABN Books is dedicated to bringing you the best in published materials consistent with the mission of Three Angels Broadcasting Network. Our goal is to uplift Jesus through books, audio, and video materials by the family of 3ABN presenters. Our in-depth Bible study guides, devotionals, biographies, and lifestyle materials promote the whole person in health and the mending of broken people. For more information, call 616-627-4651 or visit 3ABN's Web site: www.3ABN.org.

Library of Congress Cataloging-in-Publication Data:

Neal, Joyce, 1945-
  Little cabin by the river : stories from Grandma Joyce / Joyce Neal.
     p. cm.
  ISBN 13: 978-0-8163-2452-1 (pbk.)
  ISBN 10: 0-8163-2452-2 (pbk.)
  I. Title.
  PZ7.N252Li 2011
  —dc22
                                                                    2011009880

11 12 13 14 15 • 5 4 3 2 1

Dedication

This book is dedicated to Momma, Helen Miner, in gratitude for her effort to raise her three children well under some very wild and primitive conditions. No matter what happened, she *never* gave up, she *never* gave in, and she *always* did her best!

For your love, guidance, and perseverance—my eternal thanks. Momma, you did well, and I love you!

Acknowledgments

I want to express my love and gratitude to the dear folks who have helped, in so many ways, to drag this little book out of me!

First off, there is Stu-y, my patient and adorable husband, who listened and encouraged me at every step, who read all the stories and laughed in all the right places! Thank you, dear.

Then there is Momma, who cheered me on all the way, who read, edited and laughed as she relived each adventure of this rag-tag collection of childish escapades.

Of course, the *real* powerhouse behind this whole project is Bobby Davis, my friend and editor at 3ABN. He's *always* coming up with new ideas for me to try, luring me forward to expand my repertoire of talents to use for God's glory.

Mary King has put many hours of research into each one of her realistic illustrations and I'm so grateful for her willingness to recapture the scenes of my childhood with accuracy. Working with her has been such a pleasure.

Then, to all the folks at my home church, who have patiently read the stories, given their expert advice, and encouraged me along the path of writing my first book, thank you! But very special thanks goes to all the KIDS who've read the stories and told me what they thought. Your help has been a treasure-house for me!

And Kristin Phillips, age twelve, has my undying gratitude for her cheerful and devoted work over a period of several weeks. She read every story and drew lots of lovely, and some very funny illustrations. I consider her to be a friend for life!

Contents

Chapter 1

Little Cabin by the River

Have you heard the rumor? Everybody is talking about it, and wondering if it's true! Somebody said that grandmas are really just antique little girls, and I suspect they may be right!

You see, I'm a grandma now, but there's a little girl living in my heart who loves adventure and fun. I'll do almost anything for a thrill. And I'll investigate everything that catches my interest, because I'm still just a kid at heart!

My love of adventure got me into some pretty alarming situations as I grew up. But it also filled my early years with rollicking good times and wide-eyed wonder as I explored my world. Why don't you curl up beside me as I tell you stories from the olden days, when once upon a time . . .

Cozy

Our little cabin perched by the side of the road like an old man watching the world pass by. It was aged to a deep brown color and hunched low to the ground. It was the first home I can remember.

If there had been only *one* person living there, it would have been crowded. But there were *five* of us—Momma and Daddy, of course; David, my big brother; me, Joyce; and my little brother, Mike. He was just a baby, so he didn't take up much space. But we were still very cozy under its tattered roof.

One of my first memories is getting my fingers caught in the flour bin. People today don't have built-in flour bins. Back then it was common to have them in the lower cupboards. When you pulled on its handle, it would open by tilting forward, but the bin was spring-loaded and would slam shut if you let go! Being not quite as tall as the bin handle, I had no idea about such things—and what would happen next! I was just curious and wanted to see what was in there.

So I pulled with all my might and stared into the open bin. Then I must have relaxed my grip, because the next thing I knew, I was in terrible pain! All of my fingers were trapped in the flour bin! Momma quickly rescued me, kissing each and every little finger. They still throbbed for a long time.

While we lived there, Daddy worked at a little sawmill during the day, while Momma cooked, cleaned, and took care of us. At night Daddy would come home all sawdust-y and smelling of pine and fir trees. The first thing he wanted to do was to take a swim in the little river that ran beyond our cabin.

Sometimes he would take along his fishing pole and return with several big trout or even a salmon for supper! Daddy was a good provider for his family. In the fall he would take his rifle and hunt a deer. Of course our family couldn't eat it all, so Daddy would share with his brothers and sister who lived nearby.

Lost and found

Well, one summer day Daddy returned from the mill and grabbed his fishing pole as usual.

"Let me go! Please let me go too!" I begged.

Poor Daddy. He just wanted to relax a little before supper, but there would be none of that if he let me tag along. When he wavered for a moment, Momma chimed in, "Aw, Everett. Let her go this time."

Daddy gave in, but he warned me I'd have to walk fast to keep up with him. That was easy to do while we crossed the driveway and the pasture where the grass was short. But as we got closer to the river, the grass and weeds were taller. Willow trees grew thickly in the low, damp places, and they sent out shoots everywhere.

I loved the smell of the river. It was fresh and musty at the same time! Did you know that willow shoots smell delicious when you run your hand along their whole length and pull off the leaves in your palm? They have a green-y smell with a hint of bitter in it. That's what I was doing as I followed the path of flattened grass where Daddy had stepped. But he hurried on while I had to stop and inhale the aromas over and over.

Then there was the enticing mud! I made little pools where my feet stood and watched the water skippers scatter when I walked. Stomping made the mud splatter in all directions, and when I pulled my shoes out slowly, it made a slurping sound. *Delightful!*

When I finally looked up, Daddy was gone!

Hmmm. Which way did he go? I couldn't tell; it all looked the same to me. I was shorter than the tallest weeds, and the willow sprouts seemed like a forest of redwoods!

"Daddy?" I called tentatively.

No answer.

"Daddy!" I cried out louder this time.

"Dad-deeeeeee!" I wailed, terrified. *I'm lost forever and will die out here by the river!* I thought. *I just know it! I wonder how long I can survive if I make a shelter out of the willow bark and branches?*

Then a beautiful sound: "I'm right here."

That was my daddy's voice all right, but just exactly where was "here"?

"I can't see you," I called, still worried.

"Just walk in my footsteps," he instructed. But the grass had sprung back up, and I couldn't tell which way he'd gone!

"Follow the sound of my voice," Daddy called. I tried to. But the weeds kept smacking me in the face. Then, as I tried to hurry, my feet got tangled up and I fell.

I started to cry, knowing I could never find my way out of this mess by myself. How I wished I hadn't dawdled and lost sight of him. Now I was lost, and who could know if he would ever find me again?

Then suddenly, a crashing noise, and Daddy was there, swinging me up onto his shoulder and carrying me away toward the river!

I stopped sniffling and looked around. How different everything looked from this vantage point! I could see where I'd fallen, as well as the pathway ahead, the river beyond, and everything! Why had I been so afraid? Looking at things from Daddy's shoulders made it all so simple!

Together we forged ahead a little farther to his favorite fishing hole. With my "help" he caught a beauty, and then we headed home for supper.

My, did supper ever taste good that night!

Heart to heart

You know, looking back on this little drama, I think of how much my daddy is like God! Since that day I've gotten lost in the weeds of my life so many times—I *really have*! Sometimes I don't follow closely enough behind Jesus, and I lose sight of Him and don't know how to get found again. But then I remember that God has a much better view of *me* than I have of *Him*—just like Daddy saw me, even though I couldn't see anything but weeds. That was because Daddy was taller. I know that God is much taller than moms and dads even; He will never lose track of where we are!

And, just like Daddy had to do many times while I was small, God will always rescue you again and again. He'll carry you in His arms all the way home! You can count on *that*!

I love you so much!
Grandma

Chapter 2

Turning Three

One breezy spring day, right after breakfast, Momma said that it was my birthday! I didn't really know what that meant, so she explained to me that I'd been born exactly three years ago on March 6. Then she told me she was so happy about it that she was going to make a cake for supper! She said that I could help her, just as soon as she could put baby Mike down for his nap.

The early morning seemed to drag by so slowly! *When will that baby get sleepy?* I wondered. I wanted him to go to sleep right away so I could bake my first cake. Momma said he'd get tired faster if I played with him, so I did my best to wear him out. But it still took a very long time!

I chased him and then had him chase me around the furniture and under the beds. I tickled him and made him laugh so hard it made his face turn red. Then Momma told me I should stop before he threw up!

"Why don't you read to him?" she asked. "Maybe that will get him settled down again." So I dutifully found one of his picture books, and pointing at each picture, I made up something I thought explained the scene on that page.

Sure enough—pretty soon Mike's eyes began to droop and his mouth began to drool. "He's ready!" I piped up with a grin.

After Momma scooped him up and took him off to his crib, she went straight to the kitchen and pulled a chair right up next to the cupboards for me to stand on. Then she tied one of her aprons around me clear up under my arms to try to keep my clothes from getting cake batter all over them.

My first cake

Momma set out the flour, sugar, salt, vanilla, and other ingredients we'd need on the countertop. Then she took out her big mixing bowl and the hand-turned eggbeater from the drawer.

First, Momma tore off two pieces of wax paper and put them one on top of the other on the counter. Then she set a round cake pan on top of them in the middle so there was wax paper sticking out on every side. Taking a pencil, she drew around the edges of the pan. When she lifted the pan, there was a perfect circle drawn on the paper. Then she handed it to me with my little scissors. "Here," she said. "Cut very carefully on the lines I've drawn, and we will put these in the bottom of the cake pans to keep the cake from sticking."

While I was doing that, Momma smeared shortening on the sides and bottom of the pans, then dusted them with flour. I tried hard to cut the circles just right, and Momma said I'd done a good job! After that, she let me sift the flour and other dry things onto another sheet of wax paper. Then she let me help her crack the fresh eggs from our very own chickens.

It was all so much fun, mixing and cracking and stirring stuff together. I didn't want to let Momma help at all! But my arm got tired from turning the handle on the eggbeater as the batter got thicker, so I had to admit I needed help before it was all over. Still, it was a joyful, happy time in the kitchen with Momma.

Seven-minute frosting

The cake smelled so good as it came out of the oven, softly browned on top. Momma let me poke a straw from the broom into the center to be sure it was done and then placed the layers carefully onto wire racks to cool while she made the frosting.

The popular recipe at that time was seven-minute frosting. Momma said *my* cake was important enough to be topped with that special frosting! But I could only watch and not help on this part, because the frosting had to be cooked on our woodstove for—what else—seven minutes, while the cook kept the eggbeater whirling all the time to make it turn out fluffy!

When the frosting was sky-high fluffy, Momma took it off the heat and added a few drops of food coloring to make it pink! It was gorgeous stuff and tasted like cherries!

Now came the hardest part—waiting for Daddy to come home from work so we could eat supper and have some cake (in the middle of the week, even!).

Finally, late in the afternoon, Daddy came swinging through the door with his empty lunch pail, hungry for something to eat. Supper was quickly put on the table, and Daddy said the blessing. I ate all my vegetables without complaining. But then I had to sit and watch the others still finishing their food. I wanted them to hurry!

At last everyone was finished and Momma brought the tall, frosted cake to the table. Then she did the most unexpected thing! She brought out three small pink candles and stuck them right down into the lovely frosting. She lit them with a match and slid the cake in front of me while she and Daddy sang "Happy Birthday." I was very happy when they sang to me, but I felt kind of shy, too, because everyone was looking at me.

"Now, take a big breath, and blow out all the candles!" David said enthusiastically. He was older, so he already knew everything about birthdays. I was just learning, but I inhaled until I thought my lungs would pop, and then, with a *whoosh*, blew as hard as I could to make every little candle flame go out! Everybody clapped and cheered as I beamed from ear to ear.

Cynthia

While Momma cut the cake into slices, Daddy got up from the table and left the room. He returned with a big, lumpy package wrapped in pretty paper. He handed it to me and said, "Open it!"

I tore off the paper as fast as I could. I had no idea that I would get a present too! Inside the package was a huge rag doll with yellow yarn hair and two black buttons for eyes. I'd never seen such a big doll before! She wore a pretty flowered dress and a hat to match. But the best part was that she w the same size as I was! I had to hold her under her arms when I held b so she wouldn't drag on the ground and ruin her sewed-on sho *wonderful*—almost as good as the little sister I'd been asking Momma to get for me. She was my twin!

Over the next few days we were inseparable. I named her Cynthia and dragged her everywhere with me. We ate and slept together, and we talked incessantly! Then I discovered she could wear my clothes, so I began to dress her in my outfits. Although I tried, I couldn't wear her dress. It was just too small. Cynthia was my constant playmate, and I loved her very much. She began to get dirty and her hair began to come undone, but that just made me love her even more because she was beginning to look more and more *like me*!

Chapter 3

Old Time Religion

Back in the olden days, where we lived, going to Sabbath School and church was a lot different from the way it is today. On nice days we could walk to church if we wanted to (or if we didn't have a car).

Our tiny white church was actually a one-room schoolhouse during the week. On Friday afternoons someone would push aside all the desks and fill the room with folding chairs for the Sabbath services. The teacher's desk sat on a little platform one step higher than the students' desks, and that was where the preacher stood to give the sermon.

Mrs. Randle's Sabbath School

My favorite part was the Sabbath School, of course! The grown-ups got to meet in the schoolroom because there were more of them. But we kindergartners got to walk to Mrs. Randle's house. She lived next door to the church, which was probably about two city blocks away across the prairie.

First, we would gather at church around the pot-bellied stove in the back of the room and sing the songs the grown-ups sang. After the song service, we children would follow our teachers to our various places for Sabbath School. Going to Mrs. Randle's house often turned into a real frolic. She always lined us up neatly before we left the schoolhouse. But just a few steps outside our neat little line would start to straggle. You see, all kinds of things distracted us—bugs, snakes, caterpillars, wildflowers, birds—they all required investigation. So by the time we reached the barbed-wire fence on the other side of the field, we weren't in a line anymore! In fact, we'd often be scattered all over in between the sagebrush and the tumbleweeds!

Now, Mrs. Randle was a very nice and kind lady. But the one thing she didn't like was straggly children. How did we know this? Because we had learned that if we straggled too far behind, we'd have to wriggle through the barbed-wire fence without Mrs. Randle's help—and *nobody* wanted to do that!

The big rubber band

You see, the fence wires were covered with sharp, twisted barbs that could tear your clothes, snag your hair, or worse yet, make deep scratches in your skin that stung and bled! Mrs. Randle would pull apart the fence wire so we could step through without getting hurt. But she wasn't going to stand there all day, by cracky! And if you dawdled—well, let's just say it wasn't always pretty.

Now I know it was shockingly rude, but at the time it was just terribly fascinating when Mrs. Randle held the wires. You see, she was not exactly fat; she was what people liked to say was "pleasingly plump." And that's the way I saw her too. She laughed easily and that made her eyes sparkle. She told wonderful stories, hugged us all every single Sabbath, and was a very patient, loving teacher.

But here's the thing: when she put her foot on the bottom wire and pulled the next one up with her hand, her dress would hang oddly. And in those days all the ladies had to wear dresses to church with long stockings. Ladies (and gentlemen, too) had to wear a garter to hold up their long stockings, or their stockings would slide down to their ankles!

Now the garters Mrs. Randle wore were like a big wide rubber band. She'd put the garter around her leg at the top of her stockings and rolled it down with her stocking tucked in all around it. But to my young eyes, her pleasingly plump leg looked rather like a sausage squeezed in two. I thought it must hurt terribly, and I wasn't sure I wanted to grow up if I had to wear contraptions like *that*! I was simply amazed that she still had a smile on her face, considering all the pain she must be in.

But speaking of pain, if we dawdled too long, Mrs. Randle would leave her post at the fence and lead the ones who'd made it in time across her yard, while the stragglers would panic and try to dive through the fence at the very last moment before she let go of the wires. (I *usually* made it in time!)

The sand table

In her living room, Mrs. Randle would have everything ready for us. The regular furniture was pushed back against the wall, and the sand table stood in the middle, surrounded by six small chairs and one big one.

A picture roll hung on a tall metal stand next to Mrs. Randle's chair. We don't use picture rolls much in Sabbath School anymore. Now everyone uses felt sets to help tell the Bible stories. But back then we used picture rolls every week! The picture roll was made of big sheets of paper—thirteen of them—on which the memory verse for that Sabbath was written. Each sheet had a beautiful picture printed on it that illustrated the Bible verse, and they were held together at the top by a metal clip and hung from the stand by a cord. When the teacher finished the lesson for one week, she'd lift that page and turn it over the top to the back side, and the memory verse for the next week would appear.

We were given little memory verse cards each week that looked just like the big picture roll. We took those cards home with us and collected them into sets! They really helped us to learn the Bible verses for the quarter, and they were a treat that we looked forward to every week!

I loved the sand table. You may have never seen one before, so I'll tell you how it worked. When it was closed, it looked like any other round table. But you could open it by putting your finger in a little hole on the tabletop and lifting up. Now under the top of the table was a box about four inches deep, filled with soft white sand. The cover had two halves, and when you lifted them they would fold down flat on the edges of the table, leaving the sandbox open to use.

We weren't allowed to play in the sand. Instead, the teacher would use it to help tell the Bible story. She had Bible characters printed on stiff paper, front and back, with tabs on their feet that she'd push into the sand so they'd stand upright. In a little paper bag she kept other items, such as rocks, twigs, and moss, that she'd use to represent bushes and trees. She even had a mirror to make rivers or lakes in the sand—and a real toy boat to set on the "water." Sometimes she would let us help move the Bible characters around too.

Then, when the story was over, Mrs. Randle would lift the lid and close the table so we could color our pictures on it. Next, she would ask each of us to say our memory verse for that week. As a reward, we were given stickers to paste on the front of the *Our Little Friend* magazines. When Sabbath School was over, we'd climb back through the fence and trek through the sagebrush to the church.

Sitting still

I didn't like church as much as I did Sabbath School because the sermon was long and I didn't understand it. I tried very hard to sit quietly, but I didn't seem to be made that way. My legs were too short to reach the floor, and they would start to hurt after awhile. I'd wriggle so a different part of my leg would rest on the chair's edge, or sometimes Momma would let me stand up for a while. She would take a white hankie out of her purse and roll it up to make a baby in a cradle, and that would amuse me for a while.

Then Daddy would lift me onto his lap so I could see what was happening up front. I still couldn't see very well, though, and pretty soon his wool suit would make my legs itch, so I'd start wiggling again. I think it must have been tiring for all of us, but then the good part would come as everyone stood to sing the closing song. I could stand on my chair then. I knew all the songs just like the grown-ups did, so I'd sing with gusto!

After church all the grown-ups would stand around talking. Once outside, we children could run and talk again. Sometimes somebody would ask us to have lunch with them. Other times Momma would invite another family to come to our house, and we'd have a glorious Sabbath afternoon together!

Once in a while, everyone would hurry to their own homes for a quick lunch and then meet somewhere to hike through the rocky hills, search for fossils, or enjoy a park—just like you probably do today! Some things have changed all right, but Sabbath activities still warm my heart today, just as they did way back then! How about you?

Chapter 4

From Cow Palace to Miner's Mansion

(Or How to Make a Silk Purse Out of a *Cow's* Ear!)

We needed a bigger house!

As our family grew, the little cabin became impossibly small. But there just weren't any houses available in our tiny town.

Then one day Daddy discovered an old run-down house that sat in a pasture behind a neighbor's barbed-wire fence! It had been abandoned years before, and nobody thought it could ever be lived in again. But they didn't know *my* parents!

One afternoon Daddy ducked between the barbed wires and walked over to inspect the old place. He was shocked when he discovered it was already inhabited—by cattle! They had *moooved* in when the front door had been blown open by the wind, and now they considered this shack their very own.

Daddy was pleased as he walked through the rickety old house, because in his eyes it showed some real promise (or at least a hint of promise). But he wasn't sure that Momma would be pleased. Daddy knew he'd have to clean up the place a bit before bringing her over to see it, so he set to work evicting the cows (who weren't too happy about that). Then he tried to sweep away the cow pies and tumbleweeds that filled the rooms.

Where to begin

When he brought Momma over to see the house, Daddy was rather proud of his accomplishments. After all, the floor looked ever so much better than before. But when Momma saw the place, she burst into tears! Daddy tried to reassure her, and soon he'd convinced her that with a little work they could turn this old house into a real home.

Where to begin was the issue. Should they repair the holes in the roof, or build a new outhouse? Put in new windowpanes, or chink the gaps in the plaster?

Momma knew where to begin—the floors needed another sweeping or two and then a good scrubbing *with bleach*! Then the walls and ceilings needed to be swept down, and whatever glass was left in the window frames had to be washed. Rats lived in the pantry—and between the walls—so they had to be dealt with rather firmly. And the birds roosting in the rafters? Well, they were gently urged to go find a tree.

A silk purse

Have you ever heard a grown-up say that you can't make a silk purse out of a sow's ear? Don't you believe it! God does it all the time—and I know that for a fact! I learned it firsthand by watching my parents turn that run-down heap of a house into a real first-class home.

When they were had finished, Daddy joked that it was so fancy it was a regular *mansion*. And Momma, with her sense of humor, mentioned that since Daddy's last name was Miner, the house was a Miner's Mansion!

The name stuck, and we moved in while it still had holes in the roof—and no electricity. Some windows had no glass, and we had no running water. We had no indoor bathroom, and the walls were rough and unfinished.

But we had everything we needed.

Daddy brought water from the river every day in five-gallon milk cans, and every evening he did some repairs—he filled the cracks in the walls or put new glass in the windows. Momma bought some inexpensive paper for the walls and made pretty curtains to cover the fronts of the cupboards.

While Momma and Daddy worked on the house, we kids were exploring! We roamed over the hills and the open land all around us, discovering new wonders at every turn. Sagebrush was everywhere, and we had a few pungent junipers. Sunshine splashed down on everything, and fresh breezes blew constantly, making the meadowlarks sing their hearts out! I loved the outdoors and would have gladly moved out into it if Momma would have let me. But my favorite discovery of all was the cow cemetery!

Warning!

Now, I must warn you: if you are a grown-up, you probably better not read this section, but if you're a kid, you're going to love this part! You see, Miner's Mansion was part of a cattle ranch, and when the rancher brought the cattle down from the higher meadows in the fall, some of the cows would die. It's a lot of work to bury that many cows, so he would just drag them with his tractor to the cow cemetery, where they would decompose.

It smelled dreadful but was oh so fascinating! I approached cautiously at first, half expecting the cows to jump up and run away. When they continued to lie still, I walked nearer and nearer.

Then I noticed that their skin was wiggling! *Something was in there!* I just had to know what it was, so I picked up a stick and stepped closer, still half afraid the cow would suddenly leap back to life again.

The nearer I got, the stronger the bad smell. In fact, I could hardly keep from gagging, but I had to solve the mystery! So I pushed on, my stick poised to defend myself should it become necessary.

I poked gingerly at the huge, bloated cow carcass.

Nothing.

I poked harder, and suddenly I heard a hissing sound!

A snake? No, but the tiny hole I'd made in the cow's hide was bubbling, and watery, foamy stuff started oozing out.

Hmmmmmm.

The skin was still wiggling, so I poked harder, and then maggots exploded everywhere! They flew through the air and splattered my jeans!

Now they were crawling out of the cow's nose and all over my shoes! How delightfully fascinating!

I bent over the carcass for a long while, trying to understand these strange goings-on; then I decided to go home for lunch and tell Momma what I had discovered. She could explain anything.

Of course, Momma was horrified and explained that I was never to go back there again!

Yeah, Miner's Mansion had it all—and then some. The funny thing is, even though the house had some things we wished it didn't and didn't have some things we wished it did, we were all very happy there—even Momma! We had lots of family and fun to go around, and there was love and laughter every day. Over the years, several Miner families lived in that old "mansion," and there's not a one of us who thinks of those years as anything but the best times of our lives!

You really *can* make a silk purse out of a *cow's* ear!

Heart to heart

Hey, kids, the proverb that says, "You can't make a silk purse out of a sow's ear" might sound kind of mysterious to you if you've never heard it before. But it just means that you can't make something beautiful from ugly material like a pig's ear. No matter what you do to it, it will always be just a pig's ear, and it will *never* turn into silk—or anything else.

The first time I heard this phrase it was said by a man who meant to insult someone. He meant that the other man had such a poor character that he'd never amount to anything. That was a very mean thing to say, and it *isn't* true! God can change anyone—even other kids who might seem hopeless to you are beautiful and loved by God. He sees people not so much as they are now but as they *will be* if they let Him make a few changes in their hearts. That's what I meant when I talked about our house. We just learned to look at it through different eyes—the eyes of our hearts!

Now, get out there, and see the world through your brand-new "heart eyes"!

Lots of love,
Grandma

Chapter 5

Rub-a-Dub-Dub, Three Kids in a Tub

Momma worked really hard every day, but on Fridays she had twice as much to do as we got ready for Sabbath. We still didn't have running water or electricity. Without them, every task took longer.

Because water was so precious in our house, we learned to be very frugal with it so Daddy wouldn't have to make so many trips to the river. But Friday was cleaning *and* bath day, so Daddy would come home after work on Thursdays and make several trips to the river with those five-gallon milk cans.

After supper all the shiny metal cans were lined up along the kitchen wall like soldiers standing at attention, and by the time we got up the next morning, Momma would already have a big kettle of water heating on the wood cookstove—and our breakfast steaming hot and smelling delicious!

We were too young to be of much help, but we tried. I'm sure many times we just made more work for her. Soon she'd say we'd worked enough and deserved some playtime, as she shooed us out the door. Then she'd cook and clean up a storm. By the time we returned from roaming through the hills and sagebrush, the house would be spotless and Sabbath dinner was already prepared. She was a wonder!

Our weekly bath

Late in the afternoon, when she thought she'd waited as long as she dared,

Momma would call us in one by one for a bath. We had a bath only once a week—on Friday evenings—and we grew mighty dusty between scrubbings! It was hard to keep us clean because of all the dirt outside. There wasn't a single patch of grass anywhere for us to play on, and besides, I loved the dirt and all the things we could do with it!

Mike was the first one into the big, round, silver tub. I suppose he got washed first because he was the littlest—and presumably had the least dirt on him. Then it was my turn, and Momma used the same water as Mike had used because it was so precious. I must say that I muddied the water considerably more than Mike did, but here's the odd thing—I hated trying to stay clean after my bath! It so limited my options of fun things to do.

David's turn was next, and when he was finished, so was the water! Momma would lug the washtub out the back door and pour the contents out on some scraggly plants she was trying to keep alive. They were the only pretty plants she looked at day after day, she thought, and she *needed* those flowers to survive! If they could survive in this dry, dusty country, so could she.

While we worked hard at staying clean, Momma would make supper so it would be ready when Daddy came home. Then it would be the grown-ups' turns for baths, and *they* thought bath night was a *luxury*. I could never figure that out!

Sundown worship

Now came the best part of the entire week—Friday evening sundown worship! Now, if you weren't raised in an Adventist family you might not know why this ritual was so wonderful. But it was the time when the pink and yellow sky drifted down to earth like a fluffy, soft blanket—wrapping itself around the whole world, and most especially around our little house and family.

Daddy would relax in his armchair while we would sit together closely on the couch with Momma. My legs were so short they stuck out straight in front of me, so I'd look at my toes while we sang "Day Is Dying in the West." It seemed to make the whole world stop whirling and just breathe soft sounds while God drew His big arms around us to keep us close to His heart and safe from everything outside.

Daddy would ask us to say our memory verses to be sure we could recite them the next day in Sabbath School. Then Momma would read us a story or two. I loved to listen to Momma read. She made everything seem so real—I could picture it all clearly in my mind.

Next it was time for prayers, and I would scoot off the couch and kneel by Momma while Daddy prayed. His voice was deep and soft, just like the night, and I felt warm and safe when he prayed for me. The whole world seemed peaceful and at rest on Friday nights.

Nowadays I like to think of all my grandchildren all over the world singing together every Friday evening at sundown. They sing, "Day Is Dying in the West" and think about me, and I sing the same song and remember them. Then we pray for each other—and *that* makes us family.

If you aren't already a part of our Friday sundown worship time, would you like to be? I sure hope you'll start joining us this very week! Remember—I'll have a candle in the window for *you*!

Day Is Dying in the West

Day is dying in the west;
heaven is touching earth with rest;
wait and worship while the night
sets the evening lamps alight
through all the sky.

Holy, holy, holy, Lord God of Hosts!
Heaven and earth are full of Thee!
Heaven and earth are praising Thee,
O Lord most high!

Little Cabin by the River

Lord of life, beneath the dome
of the universe, Thy home,
gather us who seek Thy face
to the fold of Thy embrace,
for Thou art nigh.

(Refrain)

While the deepening shadows fall,
heart of love enfolding all,
through the glory and the grace
of the stars that veil Thy face,
our hearts ascend.

(Refrain)

When forever from our sight
pass the stars, the day, the night,
Lord of angels, on our eyes
let eternal morning rise
and shadows end.

(Refrain)

Lyrics: Mary Lathbury. Music: William Sherwin.

Chapter 6
Progress and Panic

Daddy worked steadily day after day fixing up the old place, and believe me, Miner's Mansion needed it!

I already told you about some of its, well, let's call them "unusual features." But there were others, too, like stargazing through the roof over my bed! I kind of liked that one, but in the winter it got pretty *cold* under the covers.

Once it actually snowed on my bed. *That* was *cool*—literally!

We didn't have electricity when we moved in, either, and I liked that just fine. But Momma didn't! Without electricity she couldn't run the vacuum cleaner over the floors, cook on an electric stove, or keep things cold in a refrigerator. She had to wash clothes on a washboard, too, and that was very hard work!

The old-fashioned icebox

The only way to keep milk and other things cool was to put them into an icebox.

Have you ever seen one of those? They only have them in museums these days, but we had one in our kitchen. It's an upright wooden box lined inside with enameled metal. Ours had three doors on the front—two on the left side and one taller one on the right. The small upper door on the left was where Daddy would put a large block of ice that kept things cold inside, but over the course of time the block of ice would melt, and since it was sitting

on wooden slats, the water would drip through to a metal tray below it.

On the other side, behind the taller door, were shelves to set our food on, and a little latch on the outside kept it tightly shut so the cold couldn't get out. It was all a very neat arrangement—quite ingenious, actually. But it still wasn't as good as an electric refrigerator would have been. Momma wanted one of those just as soon as Daddy managed to rig up the wires to bring electricity into the house.

Robbers!

One night I woke up to the sound of pounding and clattering downstairs, so I crept over to the top of the stairs and peered into the darkness.

There it was again! Such a racket!

I crept down a step or two and then stopped cold in my tracks. I could hear voices! *Can they be robbers?* I wondered. I snuck a little closer and put my ear against the stairwell wall. Low voices drifted through the door at the bottom of the stairs, but I couldn't make out what was being said. *They must be trying to guess where we kept all our valuables!*

Then all fell silent again. I hardly dared to breathe.

Bang! The sound nearly startled me out of my pajamas! I wanted to dash back upstairs to safety, but I couldn't move. *Oh, what will happen if the robbers find me? I could die right here on the stairs, and no one will find me until morning! But it will be too late then.*

Then the knob on the door squeaked as it turned ever so slowly. A sliver of flickering light shone on the wall behind my head.

They've heard me! Now my life is over. I'm a goner!

The door opened wider.

It was . . . Momma, who had come to see why I was out of bed! What a disappointment. The little drama in my head was over now, and I'd have to go back and try to sleep with all that noise! But instead of sending me back to bed, Momma said I could come into the living room and sit with her on the couch while Daddy worked.

He had big rolls of coiled wire on the floor, and he was using a hand drill to tunnel through two-by-fours in the wall. I watched in fascination as it made little wood curls that fell into a heap. His arms went 'round and 'round, turning the bit. Every once in a while he'd stop and blow into the hole he was making. That made the sawdust—and the regular dust—fly in all directions. I thought it looked pretty in the lamplight, but Momma didn't!

I felt very cozy and very grown up because I was awake and my brothers were asleep. After awhile, I grew drowsy, so Momma led me off to my bed again. The next morning she said we'd have electric lights by that evening and that pretty soon she would have a real refrigerator and stove! She was so happy and excited that it made me happy and excited too.

Electric lights seemed too bright and harsh at first, but in a few days we got used to them and soon we couldn't remember what life was like without them.

Daddy said the next thing to go would be the icebox, and sure enough, in a day or two, he brought a refrigerator home! It was a fine refrigerator with a motor on top. It made a whirring, humming sound as it kept the food cold—and believe me, the food *really was cold* for the first time I could remember. It was only barely cool when we had the icebox.

Daddy put the old icebox beside the woodshed that might double as the garage if we got a car someday. Because he didn't have a way to haul the heavy icebox to the dump, it just sat there for a few days until he could borrow a car again.

The dangerous game

We cousins frequently went to each others' homes to play. All the aunts and uncles would play table games in the winter, but in the nice weather, they liked to play croquet.

Have you ever played croquet? Using a wooden mallet, you drive a rock-hard wooden ball through a course of hoops called wickets, stuck into a nice, smooth lawn. The first to return the ball through all the hoops and hit the multicolored stake at the end is the winner! Sounds simple enough, right?

Well, there are other rules, too, such as being allowed to knock your opponents' balls off course, and other dastardly schemes that lead to much merriment and rivalry! But we kids always thought it was kind of boring—unless Daddy and the uncles were the ones wielding the mallets. Then you'd better be prepared to take cover!

We liked to whoop and holler and to play more active games such as our favorite—hide-and-seek. The thrill of the hunt and the challenge of staying hidden were more to our liking.

This particular day, the cousins were at our house. We'd been playing hide-and-seek for quite a while and were running out of new places to hide when it occurred to me that no one had tried the icebox yet. Surely no one would think to look for me in there. I'd be the last one found. I'd be the winner!

I opened the tall door, crawled inside, and pulled the door shut. Just as it closed, I heard the latch on the outside fall into place, but it didn't concern me because I was too young to know I was in *real* danger this time—not like the imaginary trouble I'd been in when I snuck down the stairs a few days before.

My cousins looked for a good long time, and just as I'd imagined, they couldn't find me. But it was getting dark outside, and they got tired and stopped looking for me—just as I began to wish someone *would* find me! You see, it was getting hotter and hotter inside that icebox. In fact, it was more like a sweatbox, and it was getting harder to breathe too!

Suddenly, I realized that everything was very quiet outside. All the kids had gone into the house and left me out there alone. I yelled as loud as I could, but no one answered. Then I pounded on the door, but it wouldn't open. And there wasn't a handle on the inside!

Now I started to panic in earnest! It was so hot and stuffy in there, and I started crying and calling out for my daddy. But Daddy was inside with everyone else and couldn't hear me.

Then I thought to pray. Momma had always said that Jesus watched over us all the time. She also told me that if I were ever in trouble, He would help me if I prayed. So I just asked Jesus to send my daddy to find me, and then I went to sleep.

Meanwhile, Momma had noticed that there was one child missing when they all trooped past the kitchen table. After awhile she remarked, "Joyce isn't with the other kids, Everett. I wonder where she is?"

Something made Daddy a little nervous, so he left his game and came outside to call my name. I sort of heard him, but he sounded so far away, almost as if I were dreaming. It didn't seem real. I even tried to answer, but I couldn't yell anymore. You see, I couldn't get enough air to yell, and I was fighting hard just not to go to sleep again.

Then, as Daddy looked for me, he had a sudden, dreadful feeling he should check the old icebox. He turned and ran back as fast as he could, his hands trembling with fear as he fumbled with the latch. He couldn't open it fast enough! He yanked with all his strength, the door flew open, and I tumbled out onto the ground, dazed and confused.

I don't remember too much after that until I was sitting on his lap in the bright kitchen with all my aunts, uncles, and cousins looking at me. I was very sleepy and just wanted to go to bed, but this time Momma and Daddy said I'd better stay awake for a little while first.

I'm glad to say that I recovered from my harrowing adventure rather quickly, and I can assure you that Daddy removed all the doors from that old icebox just as quickly so no one could ever get trapped in there again. But all of us knew it was Jesus who told him where to find me.

Heart to heart

Whew! That was a *really close call* for me, but I've had many more tight squeezes in my life from time to time. I also have no doubt that *you've* had a scare or two, yourself, huh? It seems that some of our adventures get us into trouble. I just know Satan is out there trying to hurt or destroy us! He chose that job. But praise God for all the guardian angels He sends to watch and care for us every day! They hover near us in good times and bad, always ready to spring into action—even before we notice we're in trouble. That's their job! And as wonderful and comforting as that is, God is eager to send *even more* help whenever we ask.

I just *love* that, and I'll bet you do too.

I've noticed that we're alike in lots of ways, you and me. We're best friends for sure! And what's even more exciting is that God is a best Friend too. He enjoys our fun and excitement as we grow and explore His world, because He made it just for *us*!

So it will always be the three of us as best friends and with angels attending our way. Stay close, now, dear grandchild.

With a twinkle in my eye,
Grandma

Chapter 7

The Invitation

The cold wind swirled around the corners of our house. It was getting ready to snow—and I wanted it to hurry!

David was in first grade now and could walk across the field to the little one-room building that served as both our schoolhouse and our church on Sabbaths. We lived so close that he could come home for lunch, if he wanted to.

I was still in my pajamas when I waved goodbye to him that day. He put on his heavy coat, pulled down his cap low over his ears, and started out into the wind. It was blowing so hard that the door slammed shut behind him, making Momma and me both jump when it went *bang*!

The wringer washer

All that morning I followed Momma around the house and helped her with her chores. It was wash day, so we heated lots of water on the old wood cookstove. Even though we had electricity now, we still used the same stove as we had before for both heating and cooking.

Daddy had recently bought Momma a wringer washing machine to make things easier. She had broken her back in a car wreck when she was a college student, and bending over a washboard made it ache badly.

When the water was hot, Momma would pour some of it into the wash-tub, add some clothes, and plug in the machine. Then it would lurch to life and start sloshing the clothes around while we added the soap. I could stand on a chair and look down into the washer if I wanted to. But sometimes Momma would put the lid over the top, and then I couldn't see anymore.

While the washer groaned with every turn of the agitator, we'd heat more water for the rinse and get ready to run the wet clothes through the wringer. We did this to squeeze the soapy water out of them before we put them back into the washtub with clean water.

Watching an old wringer washer at work is a fasci- 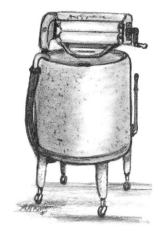 nating thing! It had a lever on its side that was like a gearshift and another one that was its brake. You could turn the wringer head of the machine to face any direction, and there was a hose attached to the bottom of the tub to drain the water out when you had finished washing.

When Momma thought the clothes were clean, she'd pull one lever to stop the agitator, and turn the head backward, facing another tub she'd set on the floor. Then, using a long stick to avoid electric shock, she'd fish the clothes out one by one and feed them carefully into the wringer.

The clothes would come out the other side looking very squashed and flat—and steaming hot! They'd drop into the tub and kind of fold themselves over while the pile grew higher and higher. Then Momma would roll the whole machine over to the sink, turn a little knob underneath, and the dirty water would run out and down the drain.

The rinse was very like the washing, except with clean water and no soap in the machine. Then Momma and I would lug the wet clothes out the back door and hang them on the clothesline to dry. It still was a lot of work compared to today's washers and dryers, but oh so much easier than using a washboard! And after they were dry, the clothes smelled deliciously like wind, sunshine, and sage as they were brought into the house, fresh from the line. And if you ask me, they smelled far better than the fabric softener you can buy today!

Anyway, that's how Momma and I spent that particular December morning. At noon, when David came home to eat a bowl of hot soup, he brought a note from the teacher to Momma. She read it and smiled.

"Well!" she said to me. "It seems that you've been invited to the Christmas party at school!"

I'd never been to a party before, but I'd heard about them! They were *fun,* and sometimes there was cake and ice cream and even presents! But I felt a little bashful because all of the kids would be bigger than me, and I didn't know how to act at a party.

Momma assured me I'd be just fine, and I started counting the days. They seemed to crawl by so slowly. I imagined over and over what it might be like, and about which dress I should wear. (Little girls almost always wore dresses in those days!)

Party day

Finally, the party day arrived, but I couldn't go over to the school until after lunch, so the morning crawled by! I thought it would never be one o'clock.

At last Momma made lunch, which I gulped down in a hurry. Then we washed my face and hands carefully, and she helped me into my prettiest weekday dress. Auntie Flo came over to watch Mike, because only the older preschoolers had been invited. Momma held my hand tightly as we picked our way through the newly fallen snow. It wasn't very deep, but it was slippery. When we reached the schoolhouse, we hung our coats on hooks in the entryway. My stomach was churning. I was glad Momma had come with me so I could watch what she did and know what to do.

Miss Millard, the teacher, had set up folding chairs around the edges of the classroom for all the visitors, so we found a place and sat down. All the big kids were talking and laughing as they finished their lunches, and I thought school must be a very fun place, indeed! Pretty soon the teacher rapped on her desk, and all the students sat down and were quiet again. She welcomed the visitors (that was *me*) and talked about Christmas and how it was a celebration of Baby Jesus' birthday. She told us about the shepherds and wise men. Then some of the schoolkids sang for us, and one of them recited a poem.

Then the door behind Miss Millard's desk opened, and a tall man stepped inside carrying a large box. It was full of gifts and red net stockings filled with nuts, oranges, hard candy, small toys, and a candy cane poking out of the top!

I wondered if all those wonderful things were only for the students, or if they might be for me too. But instead of giving the stockings away, the teacher began to pull out the gifts, one at a time, and read the name that was printed on each one. There was a gift for every boy and girl in the class—and one for me too!

I eagerly tore off the wrapping paper. At first I didn't know what it was. It was a small flat box with pretty flowers all over the lid. Inside, I was delighted to find sheets of stationery paper and little envelopes to match. There were folded note cards, sticky seals to go on the letters I'd write, a pen, and a pencil. It was lovely, and it was the most grown-up gift I'd ever received!

Pretty soon I was given a stocking, too, but my attention was on the wonderful box of stationery. I carried it home under my coat to keep it dry and safe, and I spent many, many hours "writing letters," even though I didn't yet know how to spell. I wasn't ready to use the gift, but I treasured it because it expressed faith in me, that someday I *would* know how to write. Hope is a precious thing!

Heart to heart

Do *you* have hope? I mean, do you believe in yourself? Do you think you can learn things you don't know yet? Do you think you can overcome any obstacle that pops up during your life?

This isn't a trick question, and it's not about whether you trust God to help you or not. God has already given you everything you need to succeed—and then more! One of those things is a challenge or two to spark your ingenuity, persistence, and optimism. God has put it into our hearts to conquer things, and we love to attempt the very things that seem difficult. Sometimes we succeed, and sometimes we don't, but it is important to do our best and to enjoy the challenge.

That's where all the real fun in life is. It's in the trying. You'll learn so much about overcoming your challenge. You will also have the bonus of discovering a lot of things you never even thought about before. And besides, the new things might be more interesting than the original challenge that got you started in the first place! You just never know where it all might lead someday.

Doesn't the possibility of adventure make you want to follow the road of discovery? I hope so, because I'm on that road, too—and I could use your company!

With love and hope in my heart,
Grandma

Chapter 8

Christmas at Wahkiacus

As Christmas approached, we received another invitation. Uncle Bill and Auntie Flo had invited the whole family to spend Christmas with them at their little cabin in the woods of Washington State! That was a long way away from Dayville. In fact, it would take all day to drive that distance.

Now when I say the whole family was invited, I mean all of my aunts, uncles, and cousins would be there. That meant *excitement*! We could stay for three fun-filled days of sledding, snowball fights, and snow-angel making. We would have popcorn every evening and pancakes every morning for breakfast.

I could hardly wait! I wanted to start that very minute, but Daddy said we had to wait for daylight the next morning. *Such torture!* It seemed a very long time indeed between supper and bedtime, but Momma filled the hours by letting me help pack the clothes we'd need. I climbed the stairs time after time to fetch long johns, mittens, gloves, sweaters, coats, hats, and boots from the closets. The pile on the couch grew taller and taller until I began to wonder how we could cram it all into the little car!

And just when I was sure it couldn't all possibly fit, Momma said, "That's enough packing for tonight. We'll fold our blankets and bring our pillows along in the morning." I worried, *Where will we put all of the bedding and clothes? There won't be enough room for us!*

Cynthia

Then a new worry came to mind. *Will I be allowed to bring my precious Cynthia on this great adventure?* Momma had said I could take her, *if there was room.* Right now, though, the chances didn't look very good, and gloomy thoughts filled my head as I drifted off to sleep.

I loved Cynthia. She was my "sister," and fun just wasn't much fun if she wasn't along. The next morning I dragged her downstairs for breakfast like I always did, and by then I'd formed a strategy. Rather than asking again if she could go, I'd just tuck her under my arm and hope no one would notice there were two of me! If I pretended it was settled, maybe that would make it so.

It worked! Nobody said anything, although Daddy rolled his eyes at Momma as I clambered into the back seat and sat atop of a pile of blankets. This was *perfect*! I could see out the window really well—and so could Cynthia! Now my best friend could share all the fun of Christmas with me.

At first, Momma and Daddy chatted with us as we sped down the curvy, two-lane highway, telling us everything they knew about our destination. Then we played car games until we got tired of that. Mike sat up front, Dave buried his nose in a book, and everyone else seemed sleepy or bored. But not Cynthia and me! We whispered secrets to each other so no one else could hear. And I pointed out things I noticed as they flew past our window. But the really neat thing about Cynthia was that she could read my mind—and I could hear her thoughts too! She always knew just what I was thinking or feeling without my having to tell her all the time. We could communicate with just a look.

Over the edge

Suddenly, I woke with Daddy gently shaking me awake. "Are you hungry, Joyce? Let's go eat."

We'd pulled over at a little roadside stand to get some lunch, and I quickly noticed that the scenery outside the car had changed. We were in a little town. A huge river was flowing beyond it. Daddy said it was the Columbia River and that we were going to drive across it after lunch! *How can that be?* I wondered. *I can hardly see the other side, and those houses over there look like tiny dots. Surely no one could build a bridge long enough to get across this river!*

But sure enough, after we'd eaten and driven a few minutes, a long red bridge appeared. It seemed low and flat at first, but as we got closer I could see that it was actually quite high over the water—and *very narrow!*

My heart started pounding as I wondered what would happen if we met another car coming toward us out in the middle of the scary bridge. I was deliciously afraid and excited at the same time! *It's such a long way down to the water—what if the bridge breaks under the weight of our car?* I held Cynthia up so she could see, too, and we were scared together.

I checked to see how the rest of the family was reacting. Momma wouldn't look down, Mike was too young to care, and David looked only a little while before he started reading again. Daddy told me to be quiet so he could drive and not go over the edge—and that sounded like a very good idea to me!

All too quickly we arrived at the far side and Daddy informed us that we were now in another state—the state of Washington. We were also only a few miles from Uncle Bill's cabin now, and there were more trees covered in deep snow along the winding roadway. Daddy had a hard time keeping our car from skidding on the ice, but he drove smoothly around every corner and kept an even speed up the hills as we climbed higher and higher above the river. One last turn and the dark water disappeared from sight as the forest grew thicker.

I noticed the huge snowflakes drifting down as we entered the tiny settlement of Wahkiacus and turned off the main road onto what was hardly more than a trail through a wide meadow. Then we turned and wound our way up into the trees again. It was harder than ever to drive through the drifts and icy ruts without going into the ditch on either side.

It was starting to become dark, and it was hard to tell where the driveways were. Daddy thought we perhaps had already passed the one we wanted when Uncle Bill appeared, waving his hat to show where we should turn. Uncle Carl stood beside him.

"Oh, dear!" Momma exclaimed, holding Mike tighter. Snow had covered the ruts since the previous car had driven up the steep incline to the cabin, but Daddy didn't slow down at all as he turned and made a run toward the top.

Uncle Bill stepped right behind us and started pushing on one side of the back bumper while Uncle Carl put all his strength into pushing the other side. Together we all slid our way to the top, pulling in right beside the front door.

Aunts and cousins came pouring out through the yellow warmth of the cabin door to welcome us. Everyone was talking at once. It was such a merry din I just couldn't help but laugh while everyone carried our stuff into the steamy coziness of the little house. It was already crammed. There were beds made up in every corner, and suitcases lined every wall. But Auntie Flo had saved a spot for us, and soon we were settled in.

After supper I rubbed a clear spot on the frosted window so I could see outside. It was snowing again—what glee! There would be oodles of deep soft snow to frolic in the next day. Our cousins gathered at every window to plan escapades for the next morning—until the games were brought out for the evening!

Fun and games

Of course, the grown-ups got the Rook game, but there was still Monopoly, caroms, Chinese checkers, and a whole slew of other games to choose from. Soon our cozy cabin rocked with the sounds of fun and laughter.

"Let's make some snow ice cream!" Cousin Sharon suggested after awhile. I'd never heard of such a thing, but it sounded like fun to me. Off we went to beg bowls from Auntie Flo.

We bundled up and opened the cabin door to discover we didn't have far to go to gather all the fresh, clean snow we needed. It was piled up everywhere! It had snowed so much we couldn't even see the car tracks we'd made just a couple of hours ago. *Yippee!*

Back in the kitchen, Sharon asked for some honey or maple syrup to stir into the snow, and Auntie Flo not only obliged us but also found some huckleberry syrup too! It was delicious. But we had to eat fast—or it would melt away!

All too soon it was getting late, and we had to find our spot on the floor to bed down for the night. It was *crazy!* Every bed was filled to capacity; every couch, chair, and divan had people draped over them, and the floor was carpeted with relatives! This was the most fun I'd ever had in my entire life! It was so hard to be quiet and go to sleep instead of whispering and giggling with my cousins, but after a very long time, peace reigned, and there was silence—except for our snoring uncles!

Snow, snow, snow!

What a hubbub broke out as everyone awoke and tried to find their clothes. There were blankets and pillows strewn everywhere! The mommas began breakfast as best they could, in between helping children with buttons and shoelaces and tangled hair; but eventually the makeshift beds got rolled up into corners, a delicious breakfast was served, and things settled into a sort of holiday rhythm.

Uncle Bill went to the shed and brought out two toboggans, some sleds, inner tubes, and snowshoes while our mommas washed the dishes and sat at the kitchen table to talk. After all of us cousins put on layers of clothes, we went outdoors, eager to take the first sled ride or to start a snow fort or to stockpile a huge mound of snowballs to use against our uncles later on!

Oh what fun we had zooming down the driveway by ourselves on inner tubes or lined up behind one another on the toboggan. When we'd reach the bottom we'd all lean hard to one side, trying to make the corner. We usually ended up in a snowdrift instead! Sometimes Daddy or one of the uncles would let us hitch a ride to the top again on one of the sleds or toboggans, but usually we had to struggle through the deep snow ourselves to earn another exhilarating ride through the flying white powder, screaming with delight until the inevitable wreck at the bottom!

I felt as if I could never get enough of the dizzying speed or take enough trips down the hillside to satisfy me, but soon the cold began to creep into my bones, and I'd make a trip indoors to the warm fireside to dry my mittens and socks. A couple of the other cousins were warming themselves, too, and our wet woolen mittens being dried by the fire filled the cabin with a musty damp smell. Auntie Flo had set up the indoor clothes drying rack behind the woodstove, and it was covered with wet clothes of every kind. Momma shoved a steaming mug of hot chocolate into my hand while she peeled layers of wet clothes off of me and hung them up to dry.

It seems the aunties had been discussing plans for Christmas Eve—which was this very night! Someone had suggested we should have divinity *and* fudge after supper, and now they were talking about walking to the little gas station and store to buy what they needed. However, the snow was deep and the side roads hadn't been plowed yet. Because they would have to walk about a mile to the store, they decided to make lunch first. Would they have enough time to walk that far and get back before dark? they wondered.

Chapter 9

Danger at Dusk

"Let's put the chili on to heat now," said Momma. "The men can eat when they're hungry, and we can get an early start that way." The aunties agreed and started preparing for their trip through the snow, but I had a hard choice! Which did I want more: still more sledding or a trip to the store? I hated missing out on anything, but no matter what I chose, I'd miss out on the other! However, now that I was with the aunties instead of the uncles, the trip to town sounded like more fun, so I begged to go too.

After gulping down a sandwich and a couple of cookies, we all started out for a pleasant afternoon hike to the little store more than a mile away. The snow was still deep and soft, and our boots sank down to their tops on every step. It was slow going. But the sun was shining now, and there was no wind to drive the cold through the gaps in our coats. We laughed and sang as we plunged along.

Of course I'd brought Cynthia with me, and she left a trail in the snow where she dragged behind me. When I became tired, Momma would pick up both of us and carry us a few steps since our legs were short and tired easily in the deep snowdrifts. Finally we reached the little store, stomped the snow off our boots, and hurried inside, where hot cider awaited every shopper on this cold Christmas Eve. The owner was jolly and seemed to know Auntie Flo. Momma and Aunt Lily hunted for the ingredients to make divinity and fudge that night.

This store was just like the ones back home. It carried everything from clotheslines to pickles. I had fun seeing what was on the shelves, even if it was the same things we had at home. Because it was all arranged differently, it all seemed brand new.

The long trek home

We lingered by the fire before heading home, trying to absorb the heat into our bodies to keep us warm on the long trudge ahead. Now it would be even more tiring because of the packages we had to carry, but the thought of making treats in the cabin made us happy and carefree.

The sun had warmed the snow just enough for ice to form on top of the paved road outside. I ran and slid my way over its smooth surface. But soon we came to the end of the plowed area and had to lift our knees high with every step. It was tiring work and not nearly as much fun as on the way down. We were still on the flat, crossing the meadow, when I first lost my grip on Cynthia, leaving her some distance behind in the snow. At first I didn't realize I'd dropped her, and when I missed her she was already several feet behind me.

"Oh Momma, I dropped Cynthia!"

Momma turned to look, and sure enough, there she was in a snowy heap by the side of the road. Momma sighed as she retraced our steps, bringing my beloved doll back to me.

"Hold on to her tighter," she said. "It's hard work to go back for her."

I did hold on tighter, but a little farther on I dropped her again. I guess my hands were so cold I just couldn't keep my grip, so Momma patiently returned her to me all over again.

On and on we trudged, snow filling our boots at every step and then melting inside, leaving us with freezing feet. Soon my legs got so heavy I asked Momma to carry me again. I could tell she was tired, too, but she picked me up anyway. I clung to her neck fiercely, holding Cynthia with both hands.

By now the aunties were struggling too. The icy crust on the deep snow made each step an effort, and the sun was dipping below the trees in the forest. Then suddenly I heard a coyote yip, and I shivered! I wasn't really afraid of coyotes, but I knew there were also wolves around—and I was afraid of those! *What if they attack us before we get home?* I worried. The sky and the snow were both turning lavender as day turned into wintry dusk and we hurried onward as best we could.

"This is taking longer than I thought," Auntie Flo said, taking a package from Aunt Lily so she could carry a cousin who was lagging behind. Everyone was exhausted by the cold, difficult hike. I detected fear in their voices as they decided to take a rest.

Lost!

"Let's push on across this flat part and then rest before we start up the hill," someone suggested, so we sloshed on, sometimes falling into a drift or slipping over the ruts. Momma put me down again to give her arms a rest, but the farther we went, the deeper the snow seemed to be. *Funny how it wasn't that way when we went to town.*

Momma said it just seemed that way because we were all tired now. I knew I surely was! My legs felt like lead, and I was puffing with every step. Then I realized that somewhere during the last few minutes I'd lost my grip on Cynthia again, and I didn't know what to do!

Momma was too tired to go back again, and besides, she'd warned me the last time I'd dropped her that it was the *last time* she'd go get her! But I loved Cynthia and couldn't bear to think of what might happen to her if we didn't retrieve her this time. *She'll probably be dragged off into the woods by a pack of wolves and eaten!*

I tugged on Momma's coat and pointed backward once again.

"Momma, I dropped Cynthia. May I go back and get her?"

Momma sighed as she scanned the road for a glimpse of the rag doll I considered my little sister.

"I'm sorry, Joyce," she answered, "We can't spare the time anymore. It's

46

almost dark, and we have a long way to go before we get home. We'll come back and look for her right after Christmas."

I couldn't believe my ears! *Leave Cynthia alone out in the cold to die? How could that be?*

"But, Momma! What about the wolves?" I cried. "They'll eat her!"

Momma tried to assure me that wolves didn't eat rag dolls and that Cynthia would still be alive when we came back, but tears rolled down my cheeks. Momma lifted me into her arms again and started walking to catch up with the others. I strained my eyes as hard as I could to get a last glimpse of my doll, but everything was all blurry through my tears. All I could see was snow, snow, and more snow. I buried my face in Momma's neck. The tears stung on my cheeks in the cold breeze, and I shoved my mittened hands up inside my coat sleeves to warm them a little.

Eventually we gathered in a tight knot to rest at the bottom of the hill. One of the aunties prayed for our safety and the strength to push forward—and I asked God to watch over Cynthia and not let the wolves get her. We looked at each other around our little circle, took a deep breath, and launched with determination for the final push.

Aunt Lily broke into a rousing chorus of "Jingle Bells," and we all joined her, singing with all our might. Then after we sang the regular verses, she started making up new verses and some of them were pretty silly! One after another, Momma and the aunties made up more verses until we were all laughing so hard our sides hurt.

Suddenly, we were at Uncle Bill's driveway, and before we knew it we were stamping snow from our boots on the back porch. Then the back door flung open and there stood Daddy and the uncles with their coats on—ready to come look for us!

There sure was a lot of hugging and kissing going on for quite a while after that! Everyone tried to tell what happened at the same time as we gathered around the woodstove to warm our frozen toes and noses. It all made a merry buzzing sound that felt like love and joy to me. We were together again all safe and sound, every one of us!

All except Cynthia.

Chapter 10

A Holiday to Remember

Soon the delicious aromas of supper on the table called us to gather around for the blessing. It wasn't very long, but it surely was heartfelt and full of gratitude from every one of us. How blest we were to be warm, cozy, and sheltered that wintry night!

There was still a huge pot of chili left over from earlier in the day, and the men said they didn't mind a bit to have leftovers. Aunt Jewell had stirred up a batch of yummy corn bread to go with it, and we slathered each chunk with butter and fireweed honey. Nothing had ever tasted better—unless it was the Waldorf salad sprinkled with a bit of cinnamon and nutmeg! We were famished, and every bit of that delicious food disappeared in a snap.

Christmas Eve

As soon as the dishes were cleared, Auntie Flo set the older boys to work cracking walnuts for fudge. They didn't have a nutcracker, so Gary, Ron, and Dave hunted up an old breadboard and hammers to crack the shells without crushing the walnuts. It was tricky work. Sometimes the shells shot across the room, ricocheted off the furniture, and conked someone on the head!

Of course, the boys thought this was great fun. Even though they apologized after they'd hit someone, I suspected they were doing it on purpose. When they mumbled "Sorry," they'd look at each other and grin! They didn't *sound* very sorry to me. But, in spite of the tomfoolery, eventually the fudge *and* the divinity were cooked and cooling on the back porch. Then dishpans of popcorn were made, and Christmas Eve could begin!

Games, stories, songs, and laughter filled the little cabin until bedtime. Nobody wanted to go to sleep except Momma and the aunties, who were exhausted from the long trek to the store. Daddy and the uncles had shoveled snow, hauled firewood, and played with most of the cousins all day, and they were watching the clock for bedtime too.

And that left just us kids! We never wanted to go to bed, but Momma said, "We're all tired now," and whenever Momma said that, it meant that she was tired, and we had to sleep so she could get some rest. She said it so often when we were growing up that to this day we tease her by saying it back to her when we're ready to leave after a visit!

The funny thing was that even though I didn't feel sleepy, I was already dreaming about Cynthia's predicament before my head was cradled in the pillow. But it seemed the merest blink of the eye before somebody yelled, "Get up! Get up! It's *Christmas!*"

Presents and more

Adults groaned while a dozen exuberant children danced over them and ran around the room in glee. With rumpled hair, Uncle Bill crawled on his hands and knees growling and lunging at us like an unhappy bear roused from hibernation. We squealed in pretended fright and tackled him to the floor while we mussed his hair even more. Uncle Bill didn't have very much hair to start with, but it stood on end all over his head, making him look like a wild man and causing us to scream even louder. When we'd try to escape, he'd grab us by our ankles and drag us back to tickle us until we begged him to stop!

"Stop that, Bill!" Auntie Flo moaned. "We'll never get them calmed down again!"

Little Cabin by the River

But we didn't want him to stop, even as he tried to look ashamed.

"Yes, dear," he replied, giving us a wink and a grin. His heart was always on our side when it came to fun!

Presents had magically appeared during the night and were piled in great heaps around the room, so Uncle Bill turned his attention to playing Santa. Soon toys and gifts were scattered everywhere, and people were covered with mounds of wrapping paper, ribbons, and boxes. It was the funnest mess I'd ever been in!

Soon breakfast was sizzling on the stove while kids brought armloads of shredded paper and gift boxes to the uncles who stood around the heater burning them a little at a time. I helped as much as I could, but my thoughts kept going back to Cynthia. I imagined that if she had survived the night without being eaten, she must surely be frozen in a block of ice by now.

"Can we go look for Cynthia today?" I begged.

"We'd better not try it yet," Momma answered. "The snowplows still haven't come, and it's too dangerous to try that walk again."

I knew Momma was right, but still I hoped we could soon rescue my best friend. The day passed happily enough as we played with our new toys and games, but a trace of sadness came over me when a quiet moment reminded me of my loss.

Dinner was wonderful. We had the biggest turkey I'd ever seen and enough olives so every kid could put one on every finger! *Why do they taste better that way?* I wondered. I still don't know the answer to that question, but every kid who's ever eaten olives has thought the same thing.

All day long I'd been listening for, and hoping to hear, the snowplow coming past the cabin. But it never did, and now it was getting dark again. My heart sank as I realized no more plows would be coming in the dark, either. Cynthia would have to brave another freezing night filled with howling wolves that were hungry enough to eat just about anything. Even rag dolls, I was sure.

Bedtime came at last, and even I was glad to snuggle down and be by myself for a while. I felt empty inside with a kind of achy hole in my heart. I missed Cynthia, and I feared she wouldn't still be where I'd dropped her yesterday.

Tomorrow we'd be going home, and Momma had promised we'd stop to look for her on our way back down the road. Oh, what a hug she'd get then! I'd never let go of her again as long as I lived, no matter how tired my arms got.

Jesus cares

Next morning was another round of bedlam as each family packed up their stuff (and tried not to get anybody else's stuff mixed up with their stuff). Daddy started the car and let it idle for a few minutes to get the heater going for us, while Momma thanked Auntie Flo and Uncle Bill for the good time and warm hospitality. I just said "Goodbye" as I streaked out the door and climbed up to my perch in the back seat, eager to be on our way to find Cynthia.

The snow was still deep on the driveway and on the road to the store. Our little coupe slid from side to side as Daddy carefully tried to keep us out of the ditch.

"Go slow, Daddy," I said, as I rolled down my window and craned my neck, searching the snow piles and the ditch beside the road. Momma rolled her window down, too, scanning every drift on her side of the car.

No Cynthia. Nothing but snow.

Daddy drove so slowly I could have walked faster, but he was looking too. His eyes searched for a glimpse of a fabric arm or leg sticking out of the snow. Occasionally he'd tap the brakes and my spirits would soar, thinking he'd seen something important. Then the car would creep slowly forward again—and my hopes would be dashed.

By the time we reached the gas and grocery store, I realized Cynthia had either been dragged off into the woods and devoured by wolves or been buried under mounds of dirty snow and had frozen to death. Either one was a terrible fate!

Momma and Daddy were both very sorry we couldn't find her, but I was horrified that the search was over and I'd never see Cynthia again! I couldn't understand why Jesus hadn't answered my prayer to find her. He'd gotten us safely home from our long hike. Didn't He care about little girls' dolls?

The long trip home was very sad and lonely for me. Christmas at Wahkiacus had been wonderful, but life would never be the same. Sure, I had other dolls, but they were all babies, and Cynthia was a little girl like me. I missed her painfully for a long, long time—and I still do! But life went on, and gradually the ache softened.

I still wondered about God, though. I wondered what I'd done wrong. I wondered if my prayer wasn't loud enough or if I hadn't said it right. Maybe God had gotten too busy answering all the grown-ups' prayers. Who knew?

Momma did! Momma knew everything, I realized.

She assured me that God does care about little girls and their dolls. She said that God never got tired or went to sleep. Then she told me that sometimes it is hard to understand why God answers some prayers with a Yes and others with a No, but He still loved me and would take care of me no matter what came my way.

I still didn't understand about Cynthia. But at least I knew God wasn't mad at me—and that made it easier to accept my loss. And you know what? Pretty soon I was laughing and singing again. God brought peace to my heart and put lots of other things and adventures into my life to make me happy.

Jesus *really does* care about little kids!

Chapter 11

The Phase

Mike was just a little guy, perhaps going on three. But he sure had a mean throwing arm! Momma said he was in his "rock-throwing phase," but he was, in fact, in his "throwing-anything-at-hand" phase! Nobody felt safe anymore. Daddy and Momma had both tried their best to break his habit. But Mike was still hurling things whenever he got frustrated—and he seemed to be frustrated often!

The swing

Somebody had given us an old swing set that we enjoyed playing on. However, it only had one swing. Now, with three kids who all wanted to use it at once, Momma was beginning to think it was more of a curse than a blessing!

On this particular day David was in school, Mike was down for his nap, and I had the swing all to myself. What joy! I stood on the seat and pumped with all my might, trying to see how high I could go. Then when I tired of that, I sat down, turning around and around to make the chains twist up, and then letting go for a dizzying ride. When it was over I felt a little light-headed, so I lay down across the swing, looking at the ground until the world stopped whirling. What fun!

Before I realized it, Mike's nap time was over. I was still lazily swinging back and forth when he burst from the back porch like a locomotive under full steam and headed straight for the swing!

I knew that by all rights I should get off and let him have a turn, but I wanted just one more minute, and *then* he could have it.

Big mistake!

In a flash, he scooped up the nearest rock and sent it sailing in my direction. Even though he wasn't yet three, he had pretty good aim—the stone hit me just above my left eye!

"Owwwww!" I cried as I ran into the house with blood running down my face. Mike, of course, took triumphant possession of our beloved swing!

Momma used a cold, wet cloth to bathe my eye to see what damage had been done. It wasn't too bad, but she thought I should see the doctor anyway. He might want to put in a stitch or two to prevent a scar.

With much protest, Mike was placed in the back seat of our borrowed car, while I sat in the front, holding a cloth to my head and wondering just exactly how the doctor was going to sew up my head. I really didn't want to think about it! Since the closest medical help was twenty miles away, I had plenty of time to wish I'd given up the swing cheerfully and promptly.

When we arrived, we waited only a few minutes before the nurse took us down a long, green hallway. Then she led us into a small examining room that smelled funny and was filled with lots of scary instruments. *Is he going to use those things on me?* I wondered. *I sure hope not!*

Luckily, the doctor was very kind and not at all scary as he inspected my cut. When he said I needed only a "butterfly" bandage, I was thrilled, picturing how pretty that must be. I was quickly disappointed, though, when I discovered it was just a plain brown bandage. But hey, it was better than a needle and thread!

I never found out exactly what punishment Mike received that evening when Daddy came home, but his behavior changed afterward. In fact, he hardly ever threw anything anymore—and I was much quicker to give him a turn on the swing too!

The Swing
by Robert Louis Stevenson

How do you like to go up in a swing,
Up in the air so blue?
Oh, I do think it the pleasantest thing
Ever a child can do!

Up in the air and over the wall,
Till I can see so wide,
Rivers and cattle and all
Over the whole countryside—

Till I look down on the garden green
Down on the roof so brown—
Up in the air I go flying again,
Up in the air and down!

Heart to heart

Guess what? I'm in another "phase" right now! Are you?

The truth is, we're all going through some "phase" or other all the time! For example, I'm going through my "nostalgic" phase, where I'm remembering the things that happened when I was a child. I'm also going through a "writing it down" phase to make a book for you!

Phases can be either good things or not-so-good things. They're really just times when we try out new behaviors or activities to see whether we like a new way of being and whether it works the way we hope it will. Sometimes it does, and, as you already know, sometimes it just doesn't work out at all!

If we're alive and growing, we'll always be in some phase or other, and that's great! Just remember to keep a close eye on your latest phase, and as soon as it starts to give you trouble, ditch it, and learn a better way! Never stop learning! Never mind your mistakes; just try again! And remember, I'm rootin' for *you,* because *you're* my beloved grandchild!

Hugs and kisses,
Grandma

Chapter 12
Little Finger Biters

Grandma was coming!

I couldn't remember her, but I knew I loved her from the way Momma talked. I watched Momma now as she cleaned the house furiously—everything had to be spick-and-span before Grandma arrived. Delicious aromas filled the air as Momma baked Grandma's favorite pie and cooked lots of food so she could spend most of her time with her mother.

Grandma was a spunky lady. She had set out from her home in California, driving by herself all the way to our house in Dayville, Oregon. That would take her two whole days!

A real lady

The next morning Momma told us to watch for a big black car. That would be the car our grandma was driving! We ran out to the road and looked both ways. No cars. So we sat down at the end of our driveway to wait. Once in a very long while, a car would pass by, but none of them were driven by Grandma.

At last we gave up and went back to our yard to play, but every few minutes I'd scan the horizon, hoping to see her there. Then, after what seemed like a very long time, a car turned off the main road and drove slowly toward our house, dust clouds billowing up behind. It stopped right by our porch, the car door opened, and out stepped a beautiful gray-haired lady, smiling from ear to ear!

Suddenly, I felt very bashful and shy. I didn't remember her, but she certainly seemed to remember me. She held out her arms and gave me a big hug.

"Joyce! My only granddaughter!" she exclaimed, her eyes shining brightly as she hugged and kissed me over and over.

Momma came out of the house to greet her, and we all helped carry her things inside. She had lots of suitcases, packages, bags, and boxes, and we wondered what could be in them all. As she slowly unpacked and put away her things, I watched her every move. Grandma smelled lovely—like violets— and all of her clothes were softly scented. She had real handkerchiefs, not Kleenex, and she had pretty gloves to wear on Sabbath. She was a real lady, and I was in awe.

Later that afternoon she appeared with three mysterious packages, giving one to David, one to Mike, and one to me. As the boys unwrapped their packages, they each found a bow and several arrows, a target, and an Indian headdress. The headbands had beads on the front, and feathers of many colors stuck up all around the top.

I unwrapped my package and found a little cowgirl outfit. It had a red bandana print blouse to go with a blue denim skirt and a vest with fringes all around that swung and swayed when I moved. There was even a scarf to match!

They were wonderful gifts, and we each loved what she had brought us, even though Momma said the boys would surely put out their eyes with those things! Well, the boys didn't put out their eyes, and I could hardly be persuaded to take off my new outfit—even when it was time for bed!

Singing for Jesus

The days passed pleasantly as Grandma told us story after story. She showed me how to sew and even played cowboys and Indians with us. Then one morning she pulled me aside and said she wanted to teach me a little song she loved. It was called "I Will Early Seek the Savior," and we practiced it over and over until I could sing it by heart. She explained that she wanted me to learn to follow Jesus while I was young so I would always be ready to go to heaven, no matter when He might come again. I thought that was a very good idea, especially if Grandma would be there too!

Now, our town was a very little town—no more than a few houses by the side of the highway, one gas station, and a couple of stores. But in one of those houses they kept the old people. These were older folks who no longer had a home of their own and who needed someone to fix their food and help them get around. They had wheelchairs, and some of them would stay in bed all day because they couldn't go outdoors anymore.

That must be awful, I decided. But Grandma had an idea.

"I think you should go sing for them, Joyce," she said. "I'm sure it would cheer them up, and they would just love it if a little girl like you would come visit."

I didn't know about that. I was scared to be in front of people. The last time I went up front to recite my thirteen memory verses in church I forgot them all and ran off the platform after the first one! How embarrassing! But Grandma promised to sit right beside me and to sing with me if I forgot the words.

I was still afraid, but I didn't want to disappoint my beloved grandma, so off we went—my heart pounding away and the butterflies fluttering in my stomach. I thought I might throw up at any second! *How can I get through this, even with Grandma right beside me?*

The car stopped and we got out, my legs numb and heavy. I hoped I couldn't walk and that Grandma would take me home! But alas, my legs seemed to work all right as we neared the gate.

The house where the old people lived was low and had a porch with nothing but windows. It also had a white picket fence all around the yard, real grass, and flower beds! (We only had weeds and dirt in our yard.) It was a very pretty house—and that made me feel better.

Pretty flowers grew along the front walkway, and I asked Grandma what their names were.

"Those are snapdragons, but I call them little 'finger biters,' " she said, showing me how to make them open their little "mouths," and "bite" my fingers. It didn't hurt at all. In fact, it was really fun! When every one of my fingers had a snapdragon attached to it, we went up to the door and knocked. A nice lady greeted us and invited us inside. Grandma visited with the old people for a little while, and then she got out her Bible and read to them. They seemed to enjoy this very much—but then the dreaded moment arrived!

"I've brought my only granddaughter, and she wants to sing for you!" she said.

That wasn't strictly true! I didn't want to sing for them, but I *would* sing because my grandma wanted me to. She smiled and gave me a little wink, as if to tell me she was right beside me and would help if I needed it.

I swallowed hard and began singing.

"I will early seek the Savior, I will learn of Him each day."

All the old folks just looked at me.

"I will follow where He leads me, I will walk the narrow way."

One of them started to smile.

"For He loves me, yes, He loves me; Jesus loves me, this I know."

Now most of them were smiling—and one woman had tears in her eyes!

"Jesus loves me, died to save me; this is why I love Him so," I finished.

Grandma beamed her approval, and all the old people wanted to pat my hand or have me come close so they could give me a hug. Grandma was right! They did like it! And she was proud of me.

The rest of Grandma's visit sped by, and all too soon she had to go back to California. But many precious memories come to mind as I think of that time with her. I sure hope you have a Grandma just like mine!

Heart to heart

You know, when I was growing up I thought all grandmas were more or less like mine. However, I get letters from all kinds of people from all over the world in my other life as "Grandma" on 3ABN. One of the things the older people say is that they wish they'd had a nice grandma when they were growing up. This made me realize that not everybody has a grandma who has the love of Jesus in her heart. It makes me feel really sad because mine was so wonderful. She lived to be just over one hundred years old before she died several years ago. Her name was Esta Alora Wyrick. That's where I get my middle name, only I spell it a'Lora.

We didn't love our grandma because she lived near us and we could see her all the time; in fact, she lived many hundreds of miles away.

We didn't love her because she had lots of money to buy us gifts. She didn't.

We loved her because we *knew* she loved *us*, and we were very precious to her.

I knew she loved me because of the way she'd always call me her *only* granddaughter! Of course, that doesn't mean she loved her grandsons any less. It just means she saw me as an individual. She had little personal ways of making each of my brothers feel just as special as I did.

Sometimes kids think that all families are the same as their own, but that's not true. Some kids have loving Christian parents, and some have very careless and unloving ones. But if that's the kind of family you were born into, you didn't have a choice about it. It's *not* your fault and you can't change anybody else in your family, no matter how hard you might try. Only Jesus can change a heart, and if there's somebody mean or cruel in your family, the best thing for you to do is to ask Jesus to help them become more like Him! Pray for that person every day.

Sometimes it can take a long time, though, and you might need somebody to help you right away. If someone in your family is hurting you in a serious way, please tell a grown-up you trust. If a person outside your family is threatening you, scaring you, or hurting you, you must tell your parents right away! And, if possible, find your grandma!

You see, grandmas have lived a long time, and they usually understand everything you're going through. If you don't have a wonderful grandma (or grandpa) in your life, then find one! Lots of older people would love to have you for a grandchild! I know I would!

With so much love, I can't hold it all,
Grandma

Chapter 13

The River of No Return

The Fourth of July dawned hot, clear, and dry—perfect weather for what Momma and Daddy had planned for all of us! Fried chicken had already been cooled in the fridge, along with Momma's famous potato salad, watermelon, and apple pie! Auntie Flo, Aunt Lily, and Aunt Jewell would bring their favorite dishes as well. *Yum!* What a feast it would be!

Momma sent us upstairs to get our swimsuits and wrap them in our towels while Daddy checked the air in the old inner tubes. That old swimming hole would ring with laughter today!

Daddy packed all our picnic stuff into the trunk and tied the inner tubes to the roof. We piled in, each of us kids vying for a window seat.

Of course, we didn't have seat belts or car seats like they have today. We had no safety devices to protect us if we were in an accident, and many more people died from injuries back then.

Shorty's gas station

David and I rolled down our windows so we could feel the wind in our hair when Daddy pulled onto the highway. We liked to stick our faces out the window a little way to get the full effect of the speed, and we grinned so our cheeks would flap in the wind. We thought it was like flying!

Daddy turned off the main road when we got to Shorty's gas station. It had only one pump, but that was all anybody needed, anyhow. Shorty was, well, *short*, but he was a lot of other things too! He was kind of round and had twinkly eyes. When he would come to the window and ask, "Fill 'er up?" he'd peer into the back seat to see whether there was a child along for the ride.

If he saw me sitting in the front seat, he'd wink at me as he washed our windshield. Then pretty soon Shorty would go inside his little hut and return with a piece or two of penny candy! We always hoped the gas tank would be empty if we passed that way.

Aunt Lily and Uncle Don lived just a bit beyond Shorty's. They had the cutest little boy, Dickie, who was best buddies with Mike and about the same age. They joined the caravan of relatives going to the river—four carloads of Miners chugged along the road, and seventeen pairs of eyes watched for the perfect picnic and swimming spot!

The inner-tube incident

Soon we all piled out, and all the mommas spread the blankets on the weeds and sand to make a place for lunch. But we didn't care about lunch; we just wanted to get into the water and play!

The shallow river felt so good after the long, dusty ride, and it was so hot that day. We splashed around and ducked under willow branches as we explored along the shore, but pretty soon we got tired of that and went to fetch our inner tubes.

Daddy dutifully warned us to stay near the edge of the river and not to float too far downstream. But I have to admit that we listened rather impatiently because the hot rocks under our feet were growing even hotter! Then we raced to see who could get wet first!

I felt very grown up as I rolled my inner tube along. I'd recently graduated from being one of the little kids, like Kathy, Dickie, and Mike, to being one of the bigger kids who were allowed to do more interesting stuff. So I was off to great adventure while the toddlers stayed by their mothers.

All went smoothly at first as we splashed each other or tried to float together by linking arms or holding the other kids' hands. But somehow I got separated from the group and noticed that I was gently floating down the middle of the stream—where I was *not* supposed to be.

Little Cabin by the River

Oh well, I thought, *I'll just paddle to the side when it gets too fast.*

I was having fun bobbing along with the current. I could go so much faster when I didn't have to depend on my leg power! *Whee!* I squealed.

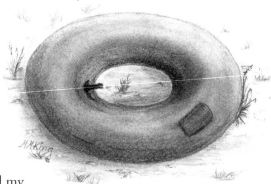

None of the other kids noticed my absence because they were having fun themselves, so I drifted farther toward the river bend where I would disappear from their sight. Then suddenly my speed picked up as I neared a stretch of rapids. My inner tube began to spin around, and I guessed it might be time to make for shore. But I couldn't! The current was too strong for me. So, according to my usual custom, I yelled at the top of my lungs for Daddy.

I seemed to be doing that a lot those days! Maybe that's why David gave me the nickname I've hated all my life. He called me Joy-beller because I was always "bellering" about something or other!

Daddy didn't hear me. I kept on floating downstream. *How long before I reach the ocean, and what will happen when I get there?* I wondered.

I was hungry too. *Will I starve before I drown?* My imagination conjured up all sorts of terrible endings!

With those thoughts swirling in mind, I thought perhaps I should yell a little louder—which I did with gusto.

Ah, sweet relief! Daddy turned and saw my predicament; in a flash he was swimming down the river toward me as fast as he could go. Then he hooked his arm through my inner tube and pulled me to shore.

He didn't scold me too much. We just walked back to the picnic along the shallow edge of the river as I held my inner tube up around my waist in the ankle-deep water. Once again I had imagined myself in more danger than Daddy did. His view of things was so much more matter-of-fact than mine. I liked mine better, though, because it was *so* much more exciting!

My, did lunch taste good! Somehow playing in the water made us hungry clear down to the tips of our toes! Know what I mean? I'll bet you've felt that way plenty of times, yourself, haven't you?

After everyone had their fill of favorite picnic goodies, we had to rest or at least stay out of the water for an hour before the grown-ups would let us go back in. They said we'd get cramps in our legs and maybe even drown if we didn't wait that long! I don't know if that's actually true or not, but it's what people thought at the time.

That hour sure went by *slowly*! We played guessing games and listened to the grown-ups talk while we waited on the blankets. They told us stories and we remembered times gone by—like the one in my next story!

Heart to heart

Of course, it wasn't really the "river of no return" for me, but it seemed that way at the time. However, sometimes in life we do come to a place where if we go any farther, things will never be the same. I'm talking about doing wrong things over and over again until they become habits.

Sometimes just one mistake can change the rest of your life! You've got a lot of life left, and it would be such a shame to spoil it all while you're so young, don't you think?

I know you don't want to do that! That's why God gave you parents— and grandparents. We're here to guide you while you're still learning about the world and about life.

I wouldn't have gotten scared if I'd paid more attention to my daddy's warnings, and while everything turned out fine for me *that time,* it was only because my father was watching and listening for my cries.

Our other Father in heaven is watching and listening for our cries too! Don't you just love Him for that? I sure do!

Lovingly,
Grandma

Chapter 14

A Harrowing Happening

As we sat on the blankets after lunch, Momma and Aunt Lily recalled a really scary story! We'd been swimming on another hot Sunday afternoon not far from where we were right then, but the river had been deeper then because the snow high up in the mountains was still melting.

Momma and Aunt Lily had been sitting on the bank, and Mike and Dickie had been playing right beside them. While they were talking and laughing at our daddies and young cousins' antics in the water, the two toddlers had slept away their nap times. And as the little boys awakened, they began playing with the sand around the edges of the blanket. They were having a good time together, trading rocks and sticks, making who knows what. When they tired of that, they rolled a ball around while the mommas made sure they kept on the prescribed blanket area.

Anyway, the mommas kept visiting while the boys busied themselves by watching the ants march across the area. They put their noses down close to the little fascinating critters, completely enthralled!

Then, a moment later, Momma turned to check on Mike, and he was gone! Totally gone—not even a trace! Dickie was still ant-watching, but Mike had disappeared!

A fear come true

Momma stood up to get a better view, but Mike was nowhere to be seen.

Aunt Lily got to her feet too. She looked around but couldn't see Mike, either. *Where could that little guy have gone so quickly?* they wondered. He'd been there only a few seconds before!

Momma started for the river, fear gripping her heart. *Surely he couldn't have gotten that far by himself in such a short a time!* she thought.

Then she saw what she dreaded the most. A little way out from the bank a little blond head bobbed just under the surface of the water!

"Everett!" she screamed, as she dashed forward. Daddy looked around quickly, but Momma could only point in Mike's direction as he floated down the current.

"Hurry! Hurry!" she screamed.

Uncle Carl dove in to try to help, but Daddy was already in the water swimming with all his might to reach his baby in time. He didn't know how long Mike had been under the water, but he knew he must get there quickly.

He grabbed one of Mike's arms, yanking him to the surface, and as he held him in his arms, Mike screamed, "Momma, Momma!" spluttering river water out of his nose and mouth. Momma said that was the sweetest sound she'd ever heard!

Daddy brought him over to the blankets and held him up by his heels to help get the water out of his lungs. Then they laid him on his stomach and rubbed his back until no more water came out.

What a narrow escape that had been! We could all smile about it, but that day had given both my of parents a terrible fright.

By the time the grown-ups had finished retelling this story, and another one or two, the hour had gone by. Then we kids ran pell-mell back into the river to swim and splash some more until it was time to pack up and go home.

It had been the perfect Fourth of July, but the day was far from being over. The most exciting part was yet to come!

Chapter 15
The Frantic Firework Fiasco

It was late in the afternoon when all the little Miners piled back into their assorted jalopies for the ride home after a long, joyful day at the river. We were all a little tired, but not as tired as our parents might *wish* we were. We still had a lot of life left in us!

Everyone came to our house to finish out the day. The mothers put out the picnic leftovers and sandwich makings so we could help ourselves whenever we got hungry again. Then they went outside to join the men for a rousing game of croquet.

Now, you may not think croquet is a very exciting pastime, but that would only be if you'd never seen my aunts and uncles play! Every game was hotly contested—with a great deal of laughter thrown in for good measure. Their games could last a couple of hours or more, and while they amused themselves this way, we cousins had a few games of our own we liked to play!

The show in the sky

The evening passed happily into dusk. This was the time we'd all been waiting for. Fireworks! What would a Fourth of July be without them?

Each family had brought a few of their favorites, and we'd put them all together to make a big show we could all enjoy.

The place we chose to set off the fireworks was up a little hill behind Miner's Mansion. There was an old cemetery up there enclosed with a wire

fence. Beside it was a place to park cars when somebody was buried, and it seemed the perfect spot. So, up the hill we trudged, the men leading the way, the cousins strung out along the dusty road in the middle, and the mommas bringing up the rear. It was still light enough to see; the sky was streaked with red and gold, and a warm, soft breeze ruffled my damp curls. It felt cool and good!

Now I don't know how it is at your house, but with us, the first fireworks were always the sparklers for us kids. That kept us happy for a while, giving the night time to deepen into real darkness so we could show off the sky works later on.

We ran around making big circles with our sparklers, sometimes standing still with an arm in the air like Lady Liberty. We whooped, shouted, and sang "Yankee Doodle." The only other holiday this much fun was Christmas!

When our sparklers ran out, the men were kind of glad, because they were really just little boys at heart and wanted to hurry on to the good stuff! You know, the firecrackers, bottle rockets, roman candles, shooting stars, whirli-gigs, and fountains of sparks!

I watched as one after another of the fireworks exploded into the night sky. I jumped whenever a firecracker popped and screamed as bottle rockets screamed back at me. A wonderful cacophony of noise, light, and black powder smoke swirled around me, almost making me feel dizzy!

All the adults *oohed* and *aahed* at the beauty, while we kids danced around and clapped after each explosion!

The hideous thing!

Now, I have to tell you something about all the uncles, but especially

Little Cabin by the River

about Uncle Bill: they all liked to play jokes on each other, but Uncle Bill liked to have fun most of all! He had sparkly blue eyes that always seemed to be hiding some secret or other, and he *really* liked to tease Auntie Flo! Sometimes she would get exasperated with him, but he would just laugh and carry on. I think I never saw him when he wasn't smiling and looking as if he were up to *something*! That's why all the cousins thought of him as their favorite uncle.

Well, he was up to something, all right! He lingered behind after all the fireworks had been lit and the rest of our group was heading down the hill to go home. It was late, and we were all tired after our long, exciting day. Auntie Flo talked softly with Momma as she held my hand to keep me from tripping in the darkness.

Then suddenly this flaming ball of shooting sparks shot between Auntie Flo's feet! She yelped and jumped with fright, running one way while Momma ran another—leaving me standing still in the middle of the road.

But whichever way Auntie Flo ran, the fireworks followed close behind! She just couldn't get away from the hideous thing as it whistled with ear-splitting volume, all the while belching fire and smoke.

She shrieked and dodged, but it kept following her! Then she ran after Uncle Carl and tried to jump into his arms to escape this beast that was out to kill her! She missed him though and stumbled into the grass at the side of the gravel road. Then, regaining her balance, she careened wildly back into the middle of the group. We all scattered, of course, leaving poor Auntie Flo to deal with this fiasco by herself!

Now, I admit that it wasn't very nice of us, but we really couldn't help laughing. It was so comical to see a grown woman trying to outrun that devious firework, screaming and prancing as the thing circled around her feet! It seemed as if it had eyes and really was following her!

You see, Uncle Bill had kept back one last shooting star, intending to send it into the air over our heads as we walked home, sort of as a finale to the evening. However, what he didn't know was that it was a dud and wasn't going to work properly. When he lit the fuse, the thing just sat there fizzling for a moment or two—and then it zoomed off at a crazy angle close to the ground. That's when all the fun started, but by then there was nothing he could do about it except hope nobody got hurt!

Well, nobody *did* get hurt—unless you count Auntie Flo's feelings—and after the thing died its natural death and she had time to collect her wits again, even she had to admit that it must have looked pretty funny!

It really was the perfect ending to a perfect day filled with adventure, laughter, and memories to last a lifetime. Aren't families great?

And speaking of fireworks, here's a little poem I like.

Heart to heart

Oh precious grandchild, as much fun as fireworks are, they're *nothing* compared to the wonderful sights and sounds of Jesus' second coming! Can you imagine how much better that will be? The Bible says that nothing our eyes have ever seen, or our ears have ever heard, or anything we could ever imagine will be as good as what God has planned for us. What a beautiful future that will be!

Have you seen any of the photographs taken from the Hubble Space Telescope? I have, and they take my breath away! However, what we see there is just a tiny glimpse—a peep through the curtain—at what God has created! And believe me, He has really put His whole heart and mind into getting our "welcome-home party" ready for us. The "fireworks" when He comes are just the beginning of it all!

Don't you get excited just thinking about it? I sure do! Let's make a promise to each other to stay close to Jesus every day so when the party starts, we'll be ready!

With lots of love for you,
Grandma

Chapter 16

Secrets in the Cellar

It was hardly more than a mound of earth behind Miner's Mansion, but it held an unexplainable attraction for Mike and me! Of course, the fact that it was dirt automatically made it irresistible. But there was more.

It had a slanted door on one side that lay snug against the earth. The one tiny windowpane in its center was so crusted with dirt and spiderwebs you couldn't see through it. Oh yes, there were mysteries in that cellar. We were sure that many secrets crouched in the dark, cool dampness of that structure. But we were also terrified to open the door and explore in the darkness.

For several weeks we were content to use it as the foundation of cities and towns, streets and highways for our cars and trucks. We'd build houses out of sticks; then we'd landscape their little yards with shrubs made from weeds. We made pretend stores from oatmeal boxes and used big empty juice cans for silos on our farms. The small cans were set up as pumps at our gas station, and Mike would use his toy road grader to carve winding roads up and down the sides of the half-buried cellar.

I had my very own fleet of cars, but not a truck or any piece of farm equipment in the lot. So I was always at a severe disadvantage when it came to building our little community. But never mind that—my hands worked just as well. And besides, I liked the feel of good clean dirt on my skin!

The dusty door

One day, however, plain old dirt just didn't hold my interest as it once had, so I ventured down the cutout dirt steps and tried to peer through the crusty windowpane.

The door was very short, but I still wasn't tall enough to see inside. Momma always said I had long legs, so that couldn't be the problem! *Well, what do I do now?* I wondered.

Mike and I consulted together and finally decided the best way to see inside was for me to lift him up and let him check things out. So down we went again. I knew I could lift his weight because he always had to be the baby when my friend Dorothy came over to play house with me. Mike hated that, by the way, but we were bigger than he was and we told him he couldn't play at all if he wasn't the baby. So he generally gave in and got toted here and there, as all good babies do.

First, we had to get rid of the pile of tumbleweeds that blocked the dusty door. I tried stomping on them to crush them into twigs. It worked pretty well, but some of the branches got stuck up under my pant legs! They were very "stickery" and made me itch like crazy, but that was the price of discovery and adventure. And the lure of the unknown drove me onward in spite of the irritations.

Once the weeds had been trampled into powder, I bent over and grabbed Mike by his knees to heft him up to window level. But I'd never tried to lift him so high before, and I began staggering around under his weight! Of course, he couldn't see much that way, so I told him to grab the window frame. That steadied us a bit, but he still couldn't see through the glass because it was so filthy.

We sat down to figure out a way to determine the cellar's contents without actually going inside. You see, outside I felt perfectly safe and brave, but who knew what lurked in the darkness beyond. It could be full of snakes and spiders! Or perhaps it was full of forgotten treasure! It could even be full of toys left there by children of long ago!

The logical solution

Then, all of a sudden, it seemed logical to me that I should try to open the door (since I was stronger) and that Mike should go inside to check things out (since he was smaller and could get away faster if he was confronted with danger). He looked at me doubtfully, but he didn't say No, either. So I grabbed the latch with gusto and yanked as hard as I could.

The dusty old hinges groaned at being forced to open after so many years of just sitting there and rusting away. The door opened only a few inches, forcing me to yank several more times to make an opening big enough to see through. Then a rush of musty, dead air hit my face. It smelled of mold, mice, and things long dead and decayed!

"OK, Mike." I flung the words over my shoulder as I continued to hold the door open. "Go see what's in there!" But Mike was nowhere to be seen! He'd wisely taken the opportunity when my back was turned and made a stealthy getaway!

Now what was I going do? The only answer was to press forward by myself, of course, but what if the door blew shut while I was inside? Well, that didn't seem too likely since it was stuck fast on its frozen hinges and the earthen floor.

Taking a deep breath first, I took a tentative step into the damp blackness. Nothing! It was too inky to see more than just a few inches in front of me at first. But then my eyes began adjusting to the new, perilous, and intriguing world.

There were two rows of rough-squared timbers holding up the roof and one larger pole directly in the center of this little hideaway room. Splintery planks lined the walls as shelves, and the floor was simply hard-packed dirt. Tiny shafts of light filtered through a crack here and there. Suddenly, I realized there were gaps in the boards overhead and fine dust was drifting down on my head. Cobwebs hung as thick as rainclouds on a stormy day, and my heart was thumping like thunder!

The desire to run tugged at the edges of my mind, but if I gave in to it I'd never know the exquisite delight of discovery! Well-behaved little girls never made history, I thought, and I didn't want to miss a thing on my way to growing up!

Do you feel that way too? It's that indefinable "something" that drives people to dare, to invent, and to explore! What fun would life be if we already knew everything there is to know? Give me a good challenge any day, and I'll be content and busy for hours!

The mysterious sound

All of a sudden, a slight rustling sound caught my ears. It came from somewhere to my left, down low, and in a pile of crumpled papers stuffed into the corner of a shelf. Most of the shelves I could see were lined with Mason jars of home-canned fruit and vegetables and stoneware crocks of various sizes. But they were so thickly covered with dust I couldn't tell what was inside them for sure. Some of them were even leaking fluid from under their lids.

Animal traps hung from the posts—big ones, little ones, and some medium-size ones too. There were also tools scattered about the floor, along with wooden boxes and crates.

There it was again! That small rustling sound told me there was something alive in there—but this time the noise was followed by a flash of fur! It was a rat almost as big as a small house cat, and he scampered over the toes of my shoes and up one of the posts nearby as I let out a scream of defiance! He'd better not try to run up my leg! Death would immediately follow that stunt—and it would be his death, not mine!

But the rat discreetly hid himself among the thick spiderwebs hanging from the ceiling. I turned my attention back to the contents of the cellar. The crates and crocks were calling me, but they were clear across the room. The only way to check them out was to go to them, even if I was scared.

I inched closer, and suddenly a snake slithered away! *Maybe this isn't a good idea after all,* I thought. *Maybe I should go get Momma to come with me, but no, that would be unworthy of such an intrepid explorer as myself!*

Then a wild, "fangy" grin met my gaze! The rest of the skull was furry, it didn't have any eyes, and its legs dangled helplessly as it hung from the wall. But the coyote wasn't alone, either; mangy pelts lined half of one wall—their laughing, toothy jaws gaping at me!

Yeow! This was just too much for me, and I turned tail and bolted out the door—up the steps, and into the warm, fresh sunlight again! The dry air tasted so good after breathing that old, musty, damp cellar air. And there sat

Mike—happily playing in the dirt as if nothing had ever happened.

Hrumph! I thought as I marched past him. He'd never know the delicious fright that awaited in the cellar depths. Oh how much he'd missed out on that day! As for me, I couldn't wait to tell Momma all about my adventure as I scampered into the house.

Heart to heart

You know, this little tale brings a smile to my face even now as I recall how daring it seemed to be at the time. Everything was bigger and unexplored territory for my growing mind and body back then. But now I'm a grandma, so I see things from a different perspective. Not a better, but hopefully a little wiser (but still adventurous) spirit lives in me.

You see, parts of me never grew up! Grandmas, as everybody knows, are just antique little girls (and grandpas are still little boys at heart). There's a middle time of life when men and women are parents, and they have a very different job to do than grandparents do. Parents have to be responsible and earn money to feed their families. They have to be sure we grow up to love Jesus and that we become good citizens of our town and country. They have to teach us to work hard and be honest in everything we do too. Parents have a lot of work to do, and they take it very seriously, as they should.

But, after that time is over, lots of parents become *grandparents* and get to relax and be a child again. And they get to do it with *you!* That's one of the many reasons we grandparents love you kids so much—we *need* you, because it would look pretty silly for an old lady like me to go digging in the dirt by herself, now wouldn't it?

But, if I have *you* by my side, it doesn't seem foolish at all. Everybody knows we are just playing together, and it makes them smile and wish they could dig in the dirt too!

I just want to say, be kind and helpful to your parents and realize they love you so much that they're willing to stop being childlike for a little while so they can bring you up in the Lord. And someday, when you're all grown up, they'll laugh and play with *your* children while you're doing the grown-up thing for a while.

That's just the way God designed life to go; a season for this and a little season for that. But here's a secret: when we all get to heaven, we'll be happy and carefree, every one of us! Laughing and playing throughout the universe will be a season that never ends!

With oodles of love,
Grandma

Chapter 17

Another Christmas

Almost one whole year had gone by since the tragedy at Wahkiacus had taken Cynthia out of my life. Christmas was coming around once more. Time had softened the ache in my heart, and my other dolls had gradually filled her place in my affections. Now I was as happy as I'd ever been before.

The special expectation of Christmas filled us with joy and our house with merry excitement. Any day now, Daddy would go up into the pine forests with our uncles to find the perfect tree to set up in our living room. It would fill the entire house with the aroma of fresh evergreens and piney sap that meant Christmas was coming!

Snow lay sprinkled thinly over the sage and sand, while a bitter north wind blew wildly into the face of Miner's Mansion, seeping through the cracks under the door and around the drafty window frames. Momma wore her sweater around the house all day now, and so did I, along with thick, long, brown cotton stockings held up with a garter belt. They were not very pretty or comfortable, but I appreciated their warmth all the same!

The catalog of wondrous things

One day as I skipped into the kitchen, Momma was sitting at the table in the middle of the room, looking at the Sears & Roebuck Christmas catalog, which had come in the mail just a day or two before. She shuffled the pages as I clambered into a chair to get a better look.

The catalog was full of the most wondrous things, many of which I'd never seen before! I'd certainly never seen so many choices in one place. Why, there were at least three different toasters, and they were all electric ones too! Momma made our toast on the rack in the oven, but in the catalog was a separate gadget just to make toast!

Beside the catalog was a slip of paper on which Momma was scribbling with a pencil. I couldn't read what it said, but Momma told me she was making out her Christmas list. Then she showed me the order form she would fill out and send back to Sears when the list was finished. They would send her all the things she'd asked for by mail, and we'd go to the post office to pick up the package after it arrived in Dayville.

A package in the mail? For us? Oh, how exciting!

Momma said she had other things to do just now, but I could take the catalog into the living room to look at the pictures. Flopping down on my tummy and propping my chin up with one hand, I slowly turned each page, from the very first one right through to the very end.

Men's flannel shirts and work boots, and women's housecoats and slippers adorned the pages. Next came curtains and kitchen appliances, followed by driving gloves, seat covers for cars, batteries, and whitewall tires. But the best part came last!

At the very back of the book were pages filled with toys! Toys for babies, toys for big and little boys, and best of all—toys for girls just my age! There were games, puzzles, Lincoln Logs, Tinkertoys, and Erector Sets. Wagons, tricycles, bikes, and scooters with happy children riding them covered the pages. I saw dollhouses and miniature furniture, sewing cards, pretend washtubs and washboards for doll clothes, and wooden clothespins to boot.

Everything was all perfectly wonderful—but *one* page filled my eyes with delight. Right there, taking up one whole page, was the most beautiful doll I'd ever seen—radiant in her soft pink satin dress, white ruffled ankle socks, and little white leather shoes with straps and silver buckles! She was sitting under a Christmas tree, waiting and wishing for someone just like me to take her home to love!

Jumping to my feet, I dashed into the kitchen to show Momma the beautiful baby doll in the catalog.

"Oh, Momma, isn't she pretty?" I asked, as I held up the book for her to see.

"She's very pretty," Momma exclaimed. "And look! It says right here that her eyes open and close, and that she cries 'Momma' when you lay her down."

"That's just like a real baby," I whispered in awe. "I wish I could have a doll like that."

"I know, honey," Momma answered quietly. "We'll just have to wait and see what Christmas might bring this year. Now put away the book and come help me with supper."

The best cook ever

Momma was frying potatoes for supper, and like many times before, I pulled my stepstool over next to the stove, my own small aluminum frying pan in hand. Momma had boiled and cooled the potatoes ahead of time and now she was peeling them before dicing them into her skillet. I could have the peelings and whatever pieces of potato that clung to them so I could copy her while practicing my cooking skills.

Soon, I had a nice little mound of hashed potatoes frying on one edge of the stovetop. Taking my miniature spatula with the red wooden handle, I carefully turned them over when I thought they were brown enough. Then Momma helped me sprinkle a bit of salt on them.

Then she told me she was making scrambled eggs because we were going to have breakfast for supper. Taking some fresh brown eggs our hens had laid, she began cracking them into a bowl. She would usually let me try to crack only one by myself since I usually squashed it, but today she did them all herself while I watched and tried to figure out her secret. I took my finger and ran it around the inside of the eggshells, trying to scrape out any leftover egg white that was still there so I could make my own tiny recipe of scrambled eggs. I loved eating my own cooking—even though Momma was the best cook ever!

The little beauty

As she put the finishing touches on the table, I could hear Daddy stomping the snow off his boots in the little lean-to outside the kitchen door. It had been dark for some time already, and Daddy was getting home later than usual. Then the door was thrown open, and in he staggered with a bushy evergreen tree under his arm!

"Well, Helen, what do you think? Will this do?" he asked as he held it upright in the middle of the room.

Turning from the table, Momma cried, "Oh, Everett! It's beautiful! Where did you find it?"

"Had to go clear up into the deep snow on the job with the boys this afternoon, and there were enough of these little beauties for each of us to cut one. So we did!"

The beautiful fir stood almost as tall as Daddy's six-foot-plus frame, and Daddy plunked it into a bucket of water to "rest" until after supper, when he'd build a holder for it.

We children chattered all through supper about how to best decorate our tree, and we could hardly wait for Momma to go deep into her closet to find the Christmas ornaments from years gone by.

After we had eaten the last morsel and cleared the table, Momma left the dishes in the sink to soak while she rummaged through the dark depths of what she and Daddy laughingly referred to as their closet. It seemed to be nothing more than a narrow hole in the wall under the stairs with a curtain pulled across the opening. It was very dark in there, and it wasn't wider than a very narrow hallway. It might even have been a hallway at some point in its distant past, but nobody knew where it ended, so it was full of mystery.

Momma disappeared for a few moments and then reappeared with her hair all mussed up, carrying boxes of lights and ornaments. I thought she must have had to wrestle something lurking in the back of the closet before he relinquished his hold on the precious ornaments, so I was glad when she returned to the warm, bright living room.

Daddy and David were already working on the tree stand using some scraps of lumber from the shed. When it was finished, the tree stood straight and proud in its neat, square, hollow box.

We all watched with great interest as Daddy put the strings of colored lights on each bough and arranged them to Momma's satisfaction. When that was finished, we turned out the lamps and plugged in the Christmas tree lights to see if all the bulbs worked. We held our breath hoping none of them had burned out because if *even one* didn't work, Daddy would have to test each one to find which bulb was burned out. And if two or more lights were out it could take many hours to locate the problem! Then we wouldn't be able to do our part of the decorating until the next day. What a disappointment *that* would be!

But there was just a moment of breathless dark; then glorious light burst forth and filled the room! The lights formed soft puddles of color on the walls, ceiling, and floors. It was magical. I sat still and silent on the couch, trying to absorb the lovely transformation in the room all around me. If I made any sound at all, the magical moment might shatter and be gone.

Finally, Momma lifted a cherished ornament from its nest of crushed tissue paper and carefully hung it on a high branch. Stepping back to admire the effect, she smiled, perhaps at the memories of when she was a girl living at home with *her* momma and daddy.

Then she helped each of us take out our favorite shiny, colored ball and hang it carefully on a bough we could easily reach. One ornament after another, the ornaments found their places on our beautiful tree until all the boxes were empty.

Now came the finishing touch that made the whole tree shimmer and gleam all the brighter! Starting at the lowest branches, we hung the tinfoil icicles just so, until every single branch had a rope of silver draped over it. Of course, Momma and Daddy were the only ones who could reach the highest branches. Last, Daddy put the golden star on the very top of our tree.

As we sat in a row on the couch, we looked at the beautiful shimmering vision of Christmas—gleaming in the corner of our house between the windows so everyone who passed by on the road might see its glory and be happy too!

Bedtime

Long before I was ready, Momma helped me into my long, footed pajamas and took me upstairs to my bed under the rafters. It was very cold and drafty in my rickety bedroom over the living room. A little warmth rose from the room below, but it flew right out between the sparse shingles overhead, and the bitter cold crept in around the drafty windowpanes.

Momma had put a hot-water bottle between the sheets earlier in the evening so there was a little warm nest for me to snuggle into under all the blankets and quilts. How good it felt!

She put my chamber pot in its usual place in the corner near the nails on which my dresses hung. A chamber pot was what we used if we had to "go" during the night—especially in the winter! Some pots were made of thick china, but ours was made of metal covered with white enamel inside and out. It had a matching lid of white enamel decorated with a red stripe around the edge. The pot itself had a wide rim so a little girl could sit on it without falling in or toppling it over onto the floor. Each morning Momma would carry it to the outhouse to empty and clean it for the next night.

The long-awaited morning

Anyway, that long winter night sped by, as did several others until Christmas morning finally arrived.

Momma tried to calm us down enough to eat breakfast before opening our presents, but it was no use. The sight of all those brightly wrapped packages under and around our tree drove us into a delighted frenzy of excitement.

Daddy pretended to be Santa Claus as he gave each one of us our gifts, trying to make his "Ho-ho-ho" sound like the Santa we'd heard on the radio. And a very fine Santa he made too!

David got Lincoln Logs and an electric train set, which thrilled him to the core. Mike got building blocks and a fire engine with a real little fire hose, which set him to wailing like a siren and running his new truck as fast as he could crawl over the floorboards—all the while grinning from ear to ear and yelling, "Get out of the way; get out of the way!"

I ripped the wrapping off one of my presents and found a tea set inside! There was a teapot with its own little lid and four small plates for sandwiches or cookies. There was also an oval platter for serving, plus four sets of cups and saucers for tea. They were made of tin and painted white with tiny pink roses and green leaves on them. They also had the loveliest little handles attached.

In my excitement, I raced to gather up my dolls for a party right away, but Momma called me back, saying there was still one box behind the tree with my name on it!

Almost reluctantly, I retraced my steps as Daddy held out another large package for me to unwrap.

Oh! What can it possibly be? I wondered. The box was about the size and shape of winter boots, and although I knew I needed a pair, it just didn't feel heavy enough to be that. The bow flew in one direction, and shreds of Christmas paper fell to the floor around my feet as I eagerly tried to guess what was inside.

When the paper finally fell off, all I saw was the back of a plain gray cardboard box. But when I turned it over—I couldn't believe my eyes! There behind the cellophane window in the box cover was the very doll I'd shown Momma in the Sears & Roebuck catalog—only she was so much more beautiful than the picture had been!

My new baby

I fumbled around while trying to get her out of that box and into my arms, so Momma had to help me. Finally I lifted her out and hugged her tightly. And when I picked her up, her eyes opened and she cried, "Momma!" I knew that if I put her down again she would close her eyes and go to sleep just like a real baby, but I must admit that several hours went by before I was willing to put her down again.

I toted her everywhere I went that day, being careful to arrange her legs into just the perfect baby pose to show off her dainty socks and shoes. I rocked her, fed her, burped her, wrapped her in blankets, changed her diapers (she even had real rubber pants!) and then did it all over again and again all day long.

I'm sure my eyes shone as I said Thank you to Momma and Daddy. My heart was so full of joy, there wasn't room for anything else! My new baby was absolutely perfect, and I named her Sarah. She was more than anything I'd hoped for, and she immediately filled the role as my constant companion—just as Cynthia had done before. Jesus really had wiped away all my childish tears and given me the desire of my young heart. And you know what? He has kept right on doing that all through the sixty-some years I have lived since that time. He *never* lets me down!

Chapter 18

A Fortunate Find

Momma held out my new pink sweater to help me slip my arms into its sleeves. "You'll be glad to have this today," she said as she put on her own jacket. "The wind is a bit chilly out there." She and I were going to town!

Shopping fun

I loved going to town, especially when it was just the two of us, like today. Now there were only two stores in Dayville besides Shorty's gas station, so it was nothing like going to the mall. The biggest store was called Dayville Mercantile & Dry Goods, and it was also the most fun. On the outside it looked sort of like a long, low barn with a covered porch the width of its front. The siding was just dry, unpainted boards standing on end, and there were only two windows made up of many smaller panes of glass with a single door between them that faced toward the road.

Inside the store were clothes and tools for sale. There were shoes and guns, and big blocks of salt for the cattle to lick. There were coils of wire, boxes of nails, and kitchen brooms lined up along the aisles. Hunting trophies of wild animal heads mounted high on the walls watched every move I made.

Coming into the cavernous dark from the sunny outdoors made it hard to see anything at first, but my eyes adjusted quickly as I followed Momma to the fabric counter. The saleslady pulled down several bolts of bright cotton cloth and laid them out. Momma told me she was going to sew a dress for me and an apron for herself, and I got to pick the fabric! It was hard to pick just one, but I finally settled on a print with tiny flowers of red, yellow, and blue scattered all over it. Then I was free to wander about while Momma finished her shopping.

The place smelled of leather and starchy new blue jeans. In those days the jeans were always very stiff and longer than your legs were so they could be worn for a long time before you had to buy a new pair. When you first got them, you'd roll up the legs at least a couple of times so they'd fit. By the time the knees started to wear out, you'd have grown enough that you didn't need to roll them anymore. But if you wore jeans without rolled-up cuffs, people thought you were very poor and couldn't afford to buy new ones.

When Momma finished buying everything on her list for that store, we went across the road to Chinouth's Grocery. It was smaller than the mercantile but every bit as interesting—and smelled much better inside! It had barrels of pickles and rows of other food set out on the wide-planked floor. The three aisles were lined with canned goods, flour, and shaving cream.

Inside the glass cases were all kinds of dried peas, beans, macaroni, and other staples, while ice cream and popsicles awaited a special occasion in a small freezer.

The bread was kept high on a shelf behind the glass-front case where the cash register sat, and penny candy stood ready to tempt children who came shopping with their mothers.

When Momma bought oleomargarine, I knew that when we got home I'd have the fun of making it yellow. You see, back then margarine was sold in one-pound blocks, not in cubes or tubs like today. It was plain white and was wrapped in cellophane, but there was also a dot of liquid food dye in a little pouch that came with the oleo so you could color the margarine if you wanted to. My job was to break open the dye and squeeze it through the mass of fat until it turned a nice bright yellow throughout. That took a lot of kneading to make it look nice without any streaks, so sometimes Momma would have to help me finish. I realize now that it was unhealthful and pretty nasty. But at the time it was all we had, so we ate it with relish!

When Momma is happy . . .

After we had finished our shopping, Momma put all the groceries in the back seat and turned the car up the hill toward home. But just after we crested the rise, she slammed on the brakes and exclaimed, "Oh look! Somebody is moving out!"

Throwing the car into reverse right there on the highway, she sped backward toward the driveway of a little square white house where people were loading a trailer with furniture. She lurched to a stop in a cloud of dust and leaped out to inquire whether the house would be for rent.

It would be!

That meant only one thing to Momma—we could say Goodbye to Miner's Mansion and say hello to a whole new, more modern way of life! This house had an indoor bathroom!

Momma quickly made all the arrangements, and we dashed home to tell Daddy. I didn't exactly understand why this was such good news, but as you know—if Momma is happy, everybody's happy! Daddy was excited, too, and almost immediately they set to work packing up things, sorting out what we'd take with us and what we'd leave behind.

The next day was Sabbath, so we went to Sabbath School and church as usual. Then Daddy and Momma took us on a nice long walk in the afternoon and read stories to us when we were all tired out and ready for bed.

Sunday morning was cleaning and painting day at the new house as we got it ready for us to occupy. The boys were left with Auntie Flo, but I was allowed to go with Momma and Daddy to help. We ate our picnic lunch at noon on the blanket we brought to sit on. There were sandwiches and Kool-Aid—with cookies for dessert! They tasted so good after we had swept floors and wiped cupboards all morning, but by early afternoon the house was spick-and-span and ready for us to move in the next day!

We were surely tired, but what a celebration we had sitting on the blanket in an empty living room with the fire blazing in the air-tight wood heater. Momma carefully poured Kool-Aid into a paper cup for me, warning me to not spill it. Then she and Daddy each took a cup too.

Daddy held his glass high and said, "To the future!" Then Momma answered him back and they pretended to clink their cups together in happy laughter. Things were looking up for all of us, but especially for Momma!

Heart to heart

You know, kids, it *really is* true what I said about our mothers! They're the very heart of a home, and when they're happy, it makes everybody else happy too.

That's one reason why it's so important for you to find ways of making her job easier and lighter. Mothers spend a lot of time thinking about each member of the family and doing things to make your life safe, clean, and healthy. And the truth is that they generally spend so much time and effort on their families that they don't often have time to take care of themselves!

And that's *not* a good thing, because being overly tired makes it tough for your momma to smile when you spill your milk or lose your socks under the bed—just before the school bus comes!

Why don't you try to do at least one thing every day to help around the house that's not already on your list of chores? Maybe you could do the one thing you know your mom doesn't like to do, or just take the next step toward becoming more responsible for yourself without being asked. It'll make Momma happy, and (repeat after me) "if Momma's happy, *everybody's* happy!"

Keep a smile on your face and laughter in your heart!
Grandma

Chapter 19

Getting Settled

Moving day was always fun and exciting for me! Momma didn't like to pack and unpack everything, but she was so glad to be moving to a different house, especially since it was modern and not so drafty.

Early in the morning, Momma woke us up and gave us a quick breakfast of cold cereal, toast, and orange juice. But before our first bite of food, she gave us a teaspoonful of cod liver oil for some extra vitamin D. It tasted *awful,* but everyone knew it was good for us, so we swallowed the stuff like good children, and then took a gulp of orange juice as fast as we could to cover up the taste!

Tooth-brushing fun

After breakfast, we brushed our teeth, but not like we do today. No siree! We didn't have tooth-paste back then. We used tooth powder instead! The powder came in the cutest little metal cans, sort of like small containers of talcum powder. The cans were red and white and said Colgate in big letters across the front. They also had a funny little cap on the top you could twist one way to uncover another lid with holes in it for the tooth powder to come out. Then you twisted the lid back to close it again. And

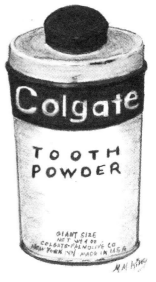

here's something interesting: since we didn't have a bathroom in Miner's Mansion, we brushed our teeth at the kitchen table with a glass of water for swishing and another for spitting!

It was lots of fun. First, I'd dip my toothbrush into the glass of water to get the bristles wet, then I'd try to sprinkle just a little bit of tooth powder onto my brush. If I did it right, the powder would stick to the brush and not fall off when I put it in my mouth. Then I'd brush around and around, finishing with a gulp and a swish to rinse quickly so I could get to the part I liked best—I got to *spit*! Without being scolded for unladylike behavior, either! I had even learned that if I did it just right, I could work in two, or maybe even three spits, before Momma would say that was enough!

Moving-day adventures

Right after breakfast all the relatives began arriving. They were going to help us move. Daddy and the uncles loaded all our furniture onto the old flatbed truck he had borrowed from his boss while Momma, Aunt Lily, and Auntie Flo piled boxes and clothes into the back seat of our car, and then they put things in their cars too.

All this excitement was especially fun for all the cousins. We dashed around trying to help, but usually we just ended up getting under foot, instead. We could carry things like pillows and towels and pack our own toys into boxes, though, and that made us feel like a real part of the action. Each time a car's trunk and seats were full, we'd all scramble for a place to sit in the heaps of assorted household items for the short trip to the new house. It didn't matter who ended up in whose car. All that mattered was finding a nook or cranny somewhere! To be left behind would have been a huge tragedy, because all the real fun was over at the new house!

There were big, empty rooms in which to dash about and closets to hide in. At first, the whole place echoed like a cavern! Best of all, the way the rooms were arranged made a circle, so we could run around and around and always end up in the same place! If there were eight or nine cousins all shouting and chasing each other through the rooms—well, I'll leave that up to your imagination! I'll just say that the bedlam we created resulted in our being exiled to the out-of-doors! No matter. Outside there was a corral and a loafing shed to be explored, and a big salt lick to be tasted! Everything was new and different, begging for us to test and try it all at once.

Gradually our old house emptied, and the other one filled up. It had been a joyous day for the children and an exhausting one for the grown-ups, who sank down into tired heaps at dusk. Then all the relatives said Goodbye, leaving us to look around at the chaos and wonder whether it would ever become the neat order we'd known before.

"We're all tired now," Momma announced as soon as the door closed behind the last relative. Momma said that a lot those days, and we had figured out it was her signal that we had tried her patience about as far as it would go and that bedtime was fast gaining on us.

Happily for all of us, someone had already made up the beds with fresh sheets, and we fell asleep almost before our heads touched the pillows. What a wonderful day it had been, and what a fantastic opportunity for exploration lay ahead for me. I could hardly wait!

Chapter 20

Hen Pecked

It was amazing how quickly Momma brought the messy house under control. Why, she almost flew around the rooms, putting dishes and groceries into cupboards, stocking the linen closet with towels, and hanging our clothes neatly in our own closets. All of this was new to us because we'd never had our own closets before—and now even the bathroom was *inside* the house! We had real cupboards with doors in the kitchen too.

While all this was going on, I set out to explore my new kingdom. I'd barely scratched the surface of discovery the day before with all the cousins around. Now I set out, determined to poke into every nook and cranny until I knew every inch of the place.

The corral drew me irresistibly, though I didn't know why. To all appearances it was deserted of life. There certainly weren't any cows, horses, or anything of any size I could chase, ride, or pet. I inspected the feed and water troughs, finding only a few wisps of straw and a couple of lingering kernels of wheat in the feed trough and a small but really disgusting pool of slimy water at the bottom of the other. However, dirty as it was, the water still made a great mirror of the sky over my head, and I looked into the ripples for a long time, imagining it was actually a window right through the middle of the earth and that what I was seeing was the sky over China! The only trouble with that thought was that I still looked like me; no little Chinese girl stared back at me from the pool.

My trophy mouse

Disappointed, I wandered toward the sheds and stalls lined up along the farthest edge of the corral, but halfway there, a furry brown lump caught my eye. A mouse lay motionless in the dirt, right out in the open! At first he appeared to be dead. But as I bent over to look closer, I could see his tiny chest rise and fall ever so slightly. He was still alive, and I thought I could probably capture him if I tried.

Why isn't he moving? I wondered. Maybe a hawk had dropped him on his head and he was just stunned. *I can rescue him and nurse him back to health!* Whatever the reason for his lethargy, he was mine and free for the taking.

My hand shot out to grab the wee beast before he revived and scurried away. But as my fingers closed around him, scooping up his limp little body, he suddenly sprang to life again at that same instant!

Worse yet, he seemed to be highly upset at the rude awakening from his perfectly good nap! His tiny feet clawed at the skin inside my fist, and when I didn't release him right away, he turned his head and bit the palm of my hand!

"Ouch! That hurt!" I cried. Then, without thinking, I threw him to the ground as hard as I could, causing him to lapse into unconsciousness again!

The wound in my palm was aching and throbbing with every beat of my heart. I could see a small, bright red pool where his teeth sunk into my hand and a little trickle of blood ran down my fingers, dripping into the dust.

Why did he bite me? I wondered. *Didn't he know I wouldn't hurt him?* At least I didn't *mean* to hurt him, but there he lay—and this time he really was dead.

Well, nursing him back to health was obviously out of the question now, but at least I could take him into the house to show Momma my trophy. She didn't like mice as much as I did. I could tell because she always took the ones she found in the house and dumped them down the hole in the outhouse! It's funny now, but I always wondered what happened to them down in that smelly, swampy darkness. I just hoped they could swim!

Anyway, I lifted my mouse by the tail and carried him triumphantly across the yard and through the back door to Momma. She was busy pushing the vacuum back and forth across the living room rug and didn't hear me come up behind her. I really thought she'd be pleased I'd killed this one myself. One less mouse would find his way into her pantry. But the vacuum kept roaring, and Momma was lost in her work. Finally, I reached up and tugged on her apron ties to get her attention.

She shut off the vacuum cleaner, turning to see what I wanted. I proudly held up my limp, bloody, dead mouse.

"Take that thing out of here!" Momma shrieked. Then she dashed toward the back door and opened it, pointing to the outdoors and yelling, "Joyce! Where did you find *that*? Oh, get him outside. Quickly! Get that filthy thing out of my house, and don't you dare drop him! You put him right back where you got him!"

She said all of this as if it were all one sentence. I was simply amazed that her breath could last that long!

Well! That certainly wasn't the reaction I'd hoped for, so I hung my head and dragged my feet through the dust on the way back to the corral. I didn't remember exactly where I'd found my mouse, but I did the best I could to put him back where he'd been before. Then I went back into the house to have Momma treat the bite on my hand.

Mommas certainly were a puzzle, though. Sometimes they rejoiced over a dead mouse in a trap, and other times they got upset by a dead mouse held up by its tail! I did think I might be a bit more careful about startling her, though. One could never be too careful about their momma's nerves!

The chicken pox

Later that evening after supper, when we all gathered for bedtime worship, Momma looked at me strangely.

"Come here," she said. "Let me take a look at you."

First, she looked at my face and neck. Then she lifted my shirt to check my tummy and back.

"How do you feel?" she asked.

"Good!" I bounced back.

"*Hmmm.* I think you've got the chicken pox."

I didn't know what that was, so I wasn't sure whether to be worried or excited. But either way, it was something new to experience. But over the next few days, little sores broke out all over me, and then they all began to itch!

Momma put pink calamine lotion on me and told me not to scratch the scabs, but it was very hard not to. She also warned me that if I did, scars would form. Then someday I'd be sorry for scratching my sores. But right then I just wanted to ease the itching.

Gradually, over the next week or so, the sores began to heal until there were only little red marks where the pox had been. Finally Momma said it was safe for me to join her and my brothers on a visit to the neighbors.

Off we went up the hill to the big ranch house where my friend Dorothy lived with her mother, father, and several big brothers. Now, by "big broth-ers," I mean that they were considerably older than I was, not to mention they were taller and quite husky in my young eyes. Why, they must have been in third or fourth grade, so they were practically grown-ups! And in fact, they seemed to think they were so much more mature and ever-so-much more sophisticated than I was.

We met Dorothy and her mother under the trees in their front yard. They wanted us to see their new calf, so we meandered over to the fence, and I climbed up on the rails.

There, on its wobbly legs, stood the most adorable one-day-old black-and-white calf. He looked so clean and pretty, and he looked different, be-cause most of the cows I'd seen were reddish-brown.

He kicked up his heels in the warm sunshine but closely followed his momma around the corral. He looked at me through the rails, and then pushed his pink wet nose against me as I patted his neck. His big brown eyes were so dark they almost seemed black—and they glistened softly under his long, curly eyelashes. I was in love!

A trying experience

But a moment later Dorothy's big brothers came swooping down from the barn. Swinging over the railings, they started chasing the cow and her calf all over the corral, whooping and hollering as they went. My wonder-ful, peaceful scene was shattered. *How can they spoil everything that way?* I wondered.

Little Cabin by the River

I glared at them through the fence, but they paid no attention. They were wild and rowdy, and I thought them quite mean. I was afraid of them, too, so I didn't say anything out loud—but I sure sent my fiercest scowl in their direction!

They kept the commotion going, glancing in my direction once in a while to be sure I was still glaring at them while they continued annoying the cow and her little calf. Finally I couldn't take it anymore! I backed down off the railing and turned to follow the rest of the group back to the shady lawn. And then something worse than being ignored happened! The boys left the cows alone, because they had lost their audience. Now they turned their full attention on *me*! They began running in circles around me, yelling wildly as before and blocking my way no matter which direction I turned.

"Yah! Yah!" they yelled as they kept me prisoner inside their tight little circle.

Then one of them noticed the red spots on my skin. Pointing to them he sang out, "Looky, looky! Joyce got chased by a chicken!"

"Yeah, and she let them bite her too!" the other brother taunted.

I was humiliated and confused. The boys yelled in singsong fashion, "Hen pecked, hen pecked! Joyce is all hen pecked!"

My face turned red with frustration and anger; tears stung my eyes. But I was not going to cry, no matter what! Looking around wildly for help, I caught sight of David, my big brother. He was my only hope, but he just stood there, separate and aloof, watching. His head was sort of down, and he seemed a little uncomfortable too. I longed for him to defend me, but he didn't. I was going to have to face these bullies on my own.

In the midst of that taunting band of brothers, I tried to think of a way out. But I was so confused and humiliated that my thoughts just whirled around and around until it made me dizzy. I couldn't focus on a single thought. All I could think of was to simply push my way through them and walk as briskly as I could toward the grassy front yard. Running was out of the question because I believed that would only make them chase me more. So, with my own head down, my fists tightly clenched, and tears stinging my eyes, I took what I hoped was a strong, confident stride forward.

Amazingly, I found I could push them aside quite easily, so I kept walking with determination and my somewhat shaky courage (even though courage was only painted on my face)!

Still trembling inside but safely back among the women, I pondered my situation. I really didn't know what to make of the charge the boys had leveled at me. I realized I was recovering from chicken pox, but I *knew* I'd never been bitten by a chicken in my whole life!

Is that really how one gets the chicken pox? I didn't think so, but how could I be sure. These guys were older than I was, so maybe they knew something I didn't. They sure acted like they knew everything!

No, I decided, *they're just mean old boys!*

Once that was decided I felt much better, but several more years went by before all my lingering doubts vanished about whether I'd been hen pecked or not!

Heart to heart

You know what? When I think about this experience, I relive the fear and confusion I felt then. Even today, I remember how much I wanted and needed a friend to stand by my side to help and defend me. I also remember the despair I felt when I realized I was all alone and didn't know what to do.

Yes, I'd been teased many times before, but it was usually by Uncle Bill. When he teased me, though, I knew he loved me because of his big smile and the twinkle in his eye. And the most fun part of all was when he'd wink at me just before he'd say something totally, outrageously silly! It was all in fun. I knew that and I loved it! But when the teasing in this story happened, it was done in meanness and cruelty—and I knew that too.

I'm pretty sure you've been in this same spot at some time or other, haven't you? I'm pretty sure you still remember how it feels to be the target of a bully with no friend in sight.

Sometimes when people are bullied, they become bullies because they don't know any better way to defend themselves. Other people react to bullying by being afraid and withdrawn for the rest of their lives.

Now, believe me, I don't know all the answers to life's hard places, so I can't advise you how to defend yourself in every situation. But I have learned a couple of things I'd like to share with you.

First of all, defending yourself isn't nearly as important as defending somebody else who really needs a friend at that moment. Be the one who steps forward to help. Become the hero to the helpless one. That's exactly what Jesus came to this earth to show us how to do, isn't it?

If somebody bullies you, decide not to let yourself become mean in return. And don't be frozen with fear, either. Jesus is always by your side to help you get through *anything*! And at the very moment you most need Him to tell you what to do, ask, and He will answer you. He's promised to do that very thing, and He will not let you down!

With so much love for you,
Grandma

Chapter 21

A Day With Auntie Flo

Her real name was Florence, but all the cousins called her Auntie Flo. The grown-ups called her by her real name. She was married to Uncle Bill, and they had one son, Gary. She lived just down the road from Miner's Mansion. Because she didn't have any little girls of her own, sometimes Momma would let me walk by myself to her house so we could do "girl stuff" together while Gary was in school.

It was a lovely spring day, and I could hardly wait to get my bed made so I'd be free to skip out the door and hurry down the road. Auntie Flo and I had big plans for the morning. We were going to spend it sewing doll clothes! I tucked my treasured doll Sarah under my arm as I listened to Momma's last-minute instructions.

"Stay clear over on the edge of the road, Joyce. Do not to talk to any strangers. Look both ways twice before crossing the road. Most important, never get into a car with someone you don't know."

Does *your* mom give you that same speech? I hope so! We all need reminders from time to time so we remember how to stay safe. Sometimes when I'm having a lot of fun, I tend to forget the things I've been warned about. Do you do that too?

A wondrous long walk

Anyway, off I went to the end of our driveway, and then I turned right and walked carefully along the edge of the highway. Very few cars ever came along that road, and not even one went by before I got to Auntie Flo's driveway.

Crossing the road after looking both ways, I started the long walk down to her house. It was set way back from the road on a one-lane dirt track. This was my favorite part of the walk because in the spring a tiny brook trickled in the ditch beside the road.

Milkweed grew there, and it smelled wet and delicious! The most wonderful, large seedpods grew along the milkweed stalks. I picked one and popped it open. Inside were wet, green seeds that weren't ready to fly yet, and the sticky white "milk" oozed out all over my hands. It tasted bitter if you got it into your mouth, so I contented myself with just pulling out the seeds one by one. A few months from now the pods would be dry. As soon as they opened, the seeds would fly away on their little parachutes!

But right now everything was green, the sun was shining warmly, and the meadowlarks on the fence posts were singing their hearts out! What a day to be a kid and fancy-free! I felt sorry for the older kids who were shut up in the little one-room schoolhouse on such a day as this.

I sauntered all along the driveway, looking in the puddles for frogs and pollywogs, and I examined the shrubs and leaves—butterflies might be about, you know!

The fuzzy surprise

Auntie Flo was watching for me and met me in the yard.

"Come see what I have," she called cheerfully.

She had something in the pocket of her apron! It was lumpy and moving around—and then it mewed! It was the sweetest little gray-and-white kitten, just six or seven weeks old. She let me carry it very carefully in my cupped hands while she held my Sarah. They were almost the same exact size, the kitty and my doll; but the kitty was warmer and softer as I nuzzled her fur.

Once in the house, we gave the kitten some warm milk. Then Auntie Flo and I pulled out her bag of fabric scraps to make a dress for Sarah. We sorted through piles of scraps until we found a piece that was both pretty and big enough to make an entire doll's outfit. We laid out the pattern on top of the fabric and began to pin it into place.

Whomp! The kitty made a flying leap right into our workspace! She was too cute to get mad at, but she sure made sewing difficult. We had to cut *very* gingerly to avoid getting her tail caught in the scissors! Then one of us had to hold her while the other one ran the sewing machine, because the kitty thought the needle flashing up and down simply must be investigated!

Eventually the doll's dress was finished. It was time for Sarah to try it on—and a perfect fit, it was. Then I wondered if it would look as good on the kitten as it did on my Sarah. Auntie Flo said we could try. It took both of us to dress the kitten without hurting her, but she looked so cute I thought about trying to trade Sarah for her! That would hurt Sarah's feelings, though, and she'd been a very good, loyal friend for a long time. No, that would never do! I loved her too much to give her up.

Auntie Flo said it was almost time for lunch and that I'd better scurry home so Momma wouldn't be concerned about me. So after kissing Auntie Flo and the kitten goodbye and tucking Sarah under my arm again, I happily retraced my steps toward home. There was so much to tell Momma!

Heart to heart

You know, when I was young (like when this story happened), I would sometimes get impatient listening to the same instructions and warnings over and over again. But it was for my own good. I know. Grown-ups are always saying that. But you know what? It really *is* for your own good.

Little Cabin by the River

Grown-ups tell you these things to protect you from danger and from getting hurt because they love you. God does that too. He inspired men to write things in the Bible to keep us safe and make us happy.

I had a wonderful time that morning with my auntie Flo, and I obeyed everything Momma had told me about being safe on the road. It not only kept me safe but made for such a fun day! Nothing happened to spoil any of my good time. It's like that with God's warnings too. They never dampen the fun; they only make it so much better!

I love all of you grandkids. Please promise me you'll stay safe and take God's words right into your heart!

With much love,
Grandma

Chapter 22

Driving Lessons

It began as a reasonably calm day, but that didn't last for long. David was in school, Mike was down for his morning nap, and I was roaming over the sun-soaked hills in the fresh air looking for bugs and butterflies. There weren't many butterflies around on this particular late spring day, but grasshoppers were all over the place. There were still a few small green ones, but most of them had turned brown and grown to medium size.

I liked to catch them and hold them between my fingers while their jaws chewed, and they spit out a sticky, brown liquid. I thought it was tobacco juice and believed that every fall they died off because they chewed tobacco all summer long. Daddy always said tobacco was nasty stuff that would kill you, and I believed him!

Anyway, I already had quite a collection of grasshoppers in one of Momma's pint canning jars. Just then I caught sight of something crawling in and out of a fresh cow pie. Bending over to inspect it, I saw lots of little iridescent-green beetles burrowing around in the dung. They seemed to be having a high old time squirming through the smelly pile, but I thought it was just plain *gross*! It was OK for flies to lay their eggs there, but it was just wrong for these pretty beetles to wallow in the stuff!

Maybe I can rescue them. But how? I wondered. If I used a stick I could dig them out, or perhaps carefully picking them up by their shells was the way to go. Either way, I needed another jar, so I started for the house to ask Momma if she couldn't spare just one more to save my beetles.

Mike's big trouble

Just as I reached for the handle on the screen door, it burst open and Mike tore past me as fast as his chubby little legs would go—with Momma in hot pursuit! He barreled straight ahead in a cloud of dust and then made a sharp right turn toward the barbed-wire fence, where he hoped to leave Momma behind and make a clean getaway!

"Don't you *ever* talk to me that way again, young man," she said emphatically as she strode after him.

Being sassy was one sure way to ruffle Momma's feathers, because Momma didn't allow sassing—*ever*! The determined look on Momma's face made it obvious that little Mikey was in big trouble! She had a hairbrush in her hand, and her long, purposeful strides indicated she meant business. And

I was pretty sure that Mike probably wasn't going to like this "business" very much!

But Mike had a very determined look on his face, too, and it was clear that he intended to evade Momma's wrath. He hardly slowed as he reached the fence and then tried to dive right through. If he could get through, liberty would be his for a little longer.

But alas! Mike's pants got caught on the wire barbs, and he hung there helplessly with his bottom in the air, feet on one side of the fence, and his head hanging down on the other. His little legs were still trying to run, but he was going nowhere.

Momma's lips curled in a wry smile as she approached her trapped prey. Justice was about to be administered! She swatted Mike on his well-padded rump while he howled in fury and continued to attempt escape. But anybody could see it was hopeless.

Eventually, Mike stopped yelling, and Momma took him down off the fence. Then she picked him up and carried him back to the house in her arms. I decided that perhaps the glass jar wasn't really that important just then and disappeared around the corner until Daddy came home for lunch.

He was driving the big tractor that day, and he parked it right outside the kitchen window. The men were mowing hay down by the river, and Daddy smelled like freshly cut alfalfa. He even had bits of it in his hair and all over his clothes, which he brushed off before going inside to eat.

Momma had a good lunch all ready, and she was smiling again as if nothing had happened that morning. Daddy said the blessing as usual, and we all talked as we ate, laughing at the funny stories Daddy told about his work that morning. Then Momma told about her day, but she never mentioned anything about her footrace with Mike or what had caused it. That meant she wasn't mad at him, and everything was OK again.

That was a relief. Life was good once more.

The wild ride

Momma and Daddy talked on awhile about grown-up stuff and I got bored, so I decided to go back outside to play. I'd forgotten the tractor was outside, but as the screen door slammed shut, I could see it standing there in all its amazing glory!

It was an old Massey Ferguson tractor, and it looked as if it might be three stories tall. It was also painted bright fire-engine red! Oh what a beautiful piece of machinery! Daddy was still talking to Momma, but I was sure he wouldn't mind if I just walked around and *looked* at it.

Its tires were huge—at least twice as tall as I was—and its engine smelled of hot oil. All the gears and levers were calling to my heart, and I wondered how it would feel to sit way up there in the driver's seat. I could just pretend to drive it, couldn't I? That wouldn't hurt anything! And even though somehow the thought just *felt* wrong, I chalked it up to excited anticipation. It was too late to resist temptation anyhow, because I already could feel the steering wheel in my hands!

Boy, was this was going to be *fun*! Where was I supposed to start climbing? I wasn't sure how to get up to the driver's seat. But by finding a toehold here and a crevice there, somehow I found myself sitting on top of the world with a steering wheel in my little hands!

I bounced up and down on the seat and turned the wheel back and forth as if I were driving over a rough, rutted field.

"Vroom! Vroom!" The sounds came from deep in my throat. In my mind, I sped over pastures, through ravines, and up steep hillsides!

I'd better shift gears too! I thought, so I grabbed the stick and yanked it while standing on one of the pedals. Then, to my great surprise, the tractor coughed once and started chugging across the yard!

Yeow! How'd that happen? I wondered, shocked and amazed at my heretofore unknown mechanical abilities! A rush of power surged over me as I realized that I really did have control over this behemoth! I could turn it one way or the other when I turned the wheel—it would go wherever I commanded it. The possibilities boggled the mind! *Where shall I go first?*

While pondering that question, I was vaguely aware I was passing the kitchen window. Momma and Daddy were still talking just on the other side. They looked up in surprise, confusion, and then terror as they watched me chugging slowly past them. And it wasn't until I saw the fear in my parents' eyes that I became concerned.

Just ahead of me the barbed-wire fence began to loom large! Yes, the very *same* barbed-wire fence that had been Mike's undoing that morning rose up to entrap me in my wrongdoing now.

Desperately I tried turning the wheel sharply enough to avoid the sure disaster that lay ahead. It wasn't just the fear that I might tear down the fence or perhaps get the tractor tangled up in the wire. What haunted me most was the image of my little brother hanging helplessly in midair while being disciplined! Now I could see a similar fate in *my* future too! Only it would be so much worse because Mike had only sassed Momma, but I was driving a tractor!

With a mixture of relief and dread, I saw Daddy sprinting toward me and the machine. He closed the distance easily and then sprang up into the driver's seat with a bound. A few swift strokes of the levers brought the tractor to a stop—just inches from the fence! We both sighed with relief as I crawled up into Daddy's lap as we caught our breath.

"How did you get this thing started?" Daddy asked when he could breathe normally again.

"I don't know," I said honestly. And you know what? To this very day I *still* don't know how it happened, though at the time I thought I was just magically gifted!

"I was pretend-driving, and it just started all by itself!" I tried to explain. Momma arrived just then.

"You could have been killed! What were you thinking?" She reached up to take me from Daddy's arms, but I couldn't answer because I honestly didn't know. So I just stood there silently with my head hanging in confusion and shame.

All was quiet for a few moments, as I felt, rather than saw, my parents stand there looking at each other not knowing what to say or do next. Then at last Daddy put a hand on my shoulder.

"Maybe the next time your curiosity gets the better of you, you should tell me so I can help you first," he said. Then he kissed Momma lightly on her cheek and swung up on the tractor again.

"I'd better get back to the field, Helen. Keep an eye on her!" he said with a straight face, but with a twinkle in his eye.

That is all? I couldn't believe it! *They aren't going to punish me!* My little soul was flooded with gratitude and relief for the gift of another chance to do better. And, believe me, I was a very good little girl the rest of that day!

And you know, even now, when I've done something wrong or foolish, that's just the way I feel when God forgives me. First, He saves me from sin and danger. Then He cancels the punishment I deserve and asks the Holy Spirit to keep an eye on me. He knows I'll surely get into trouble again without His watchfulness and care.

But the very best part is that my soul is flooded with gratitude and relief when Jesus gives me another chance to do better the next time! Oh, how I love Him for that gift—and I'm sure you feel the same way, too, don't you? After all, you're my grandchild, and we are alike in so many ways. Remember that I love you very much—just like Jesus does!

Chapter 23

Grasshoppers, Mice, and Rats, Oh My!

Sunshine lasted longer every day now, and Daddy was busier than ever. It seemed like he was working constantly and hardly had time to eat his supper after spending all day in the fields, the mill, or on another job. He'd work until dark every day, and of course, we were in bed by then so we weren't seeing much of him those days.

Daddy was building a new house for us! It sat on a little plot of land that was closer to town. In fact, it sat right on the crest of the hill that went straight down into Dayville. The land behind our new house dropped off toward the river, so we could see out in every direction.

After the foundation was in place and the subfloor was laid, Daddy began taking us over with him in the evenings. That was lots better—and so much fun! There were sawhorses to ride and knotholes in the floor to peer through into the darkness below. There was sawdust to play in and wooden curls to gather. Then I would try to make them stick to my head like ringlets.

One of the first things Daddy did was build us a new outhouse until we had a bathroom that worked. It didn't even smell bad, being brand new and all! And this one had *two* holes, so two people could use it at the same time—what a fantastic advance in technology! Before Daddy set the little building in place over the hole he'd dug in the ground, I spent a long time staring down into it, wondering whether it was deeper than my head. *If I fall in, could I get out again?* I wondered.

Over in our real house Daddy put down two-by-fours on the subfloor to show where the walls would go and then he showed me where my new bedroom would be. It was hard to imagine how it would all look when it was finished, but it sure was exciting! Day by day the boards went up until the framing was done. The rafters came next and then came the roof. By now it was starting to look like a real house!

The strange man

One day a strange man came walking over from a neighbor's house, and Daddy walked over to meet him. I was tagging along as usual. When the man got close enough that I could see him well, I decided I didn't like him at all! He was rather short, smelled bad, and had brown lips! Not like suntan brown, they were *stained* brown, and so were his teeth and fingers. He talked roughly and said bad words, and he looked at me funny. No, I absolutely did not like this man, and I could tell Daddy didn't like him much, either, because he kind of pushed me behind him and told me to go back to Momma. I was really glad to go, too, and felt much better when I was away from the stranger.

Daddy stayed and talked for a little while and then came back to work some more. He said the man was just being neighborly and wanted to greet us and see how the house was coming along. But I was afraid he would come back again.

He did come back a few times while Daddy continued to build, but I would always hide during his visits. Then one day after he left I blurted out, "I don't like that man, Daddy. His lips are *brown*!"

Daddy just chuckled and explained, "I know he's kinda rough around the edges, Joyce. His lips are brown because he chews tobacco. He's all right, though. He won't hurt you, but you don't have to talk to him if you don't want to."

Whew! That was a relief! But now I felt sort of sorry for him. I pictured him as having a grasshopper face with dark brown saliva all around his mouth, like the ones I saw chewing "tobacco" all over the yard at this time of year. I was convinced that, just like the grasshoppers, he would die off in the fall when it got cold, poor fellow! I still thought I should keep a wary eye on him, which I did for as long as we lived in that house.

Pink babies

In the meantime, every day the house looked more and more cozy. Soon the walls were up and the kitchen had a sink with running water. It must be time to move in!

It was primitive at first, but Momma and Daddy worked on it every chance they got. The floors still weren't finished, and Momma stuffed old socks into and tacked cardboard over the knotholes. The mice got in anyway and found a wonderful nest in my underwear drawer one day. They must have gone undetected for several days because when Momma found them, their nest was full of tiny pink babies hardly any bigger than my thumb! There must have been at least eight or nine of them, and I was absolutely delighted, but Momma was horrified!

Eeek! she screamed in surprise. "They've ruined all your underwear!"

Scooping up the nest in her hands and holding it at arm's length so as not to become contaminated from the wee creatures, she took long strides toward the kitchen door.

"Whaddya gonna do with 'em?" I implored, shadowing her every step. "Can't I keep them, Momma? They're just babies, and they won't hurt anything!"

But Momma strode on through the kitchen door and straight toward the outhouse.

"These babies will grow up to be dirty grown-up mice, Joyce. They'll get into the cupboards and ruin our food; they'll chew everything to pieces, just like your underwear," she continued, "and no, you can't keep them!"

I couldn't stand to look. Momma opened the outhouse door, and I just knew what was coming next! The door banged shut behind her, and all was quiet for a moment. Then she reappeared without the nest or the babies.

As I looked uncertainly toward the outhouse, Momma gently turned me toward the kitchen door.

"No, don't go looking for them. It's better this way," she said as she took me inside. Giving me something to do, she tried to take my mind off the tragedy. But soon sadness turned to insatiable curiosity. This was my one chance to find out for myself whether baby mice could swim! There would never be another opportunity for such a scientific investigation as this, and I just had to know!

Momma was busy ironing by this time and didn't notice as I snuck out through the kitchen. As soon as the door was pulled shut, I ran toward the outhouse, flung open the door, and looked down one of the holes.

In the faint light, I looked carefully for any little pink bodies, swimming or otherwise, but none were there. The only thing I could make out was the small heap of my undershirt-nest overturned at the bottom of the hole. Ah, well, life went on, and the warm sunshine called me to other pursuits as I skipped happily away, my mind already drawn to new mysteries that lay ahead.

One Sunday morning, not long after this, even *more* excitement erupted as we lingered in bed, still half asleep.

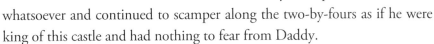

Momma and Daddy were talking quietly together in their room when a huge pack rat ventured out onto one of the exposed rafters over their bed!

Momma drew in her breath sharply as Daddy cautiously pulled out the .22 rifle he had hidden under the bed. But this foolhardy rat paid no attention whatsoever and continued to scamper along the two-by-fours as if he were king of this castle and had nothing to fear from Daddy.

Poor, misguided beast! Daddy carefully and quietly took aim. *Boom!* The entire house shook and the windows rattled. I nearly jumped out of my skin as I heard Momma shriek, "Everett!"

I dashed as fast as I could into their room to see Daddy grinning triumphantly with the .22 on his lap and Momma looking up at the rafters in shocked dismay. The daring rat was nowhere to be seen, and it was just as well—I really didn't need to know all the details about what it took to keep our home varmint free!

Heart to heart

So, how many "varmints" are living in your house? You know—all those pesky little bad habits and character flaws that seem so hard to overcome?

Momma was right, as usual, when she said those darling baby mice would just grow up to be big ones, and they would ruin our clothes. It's the same way with the wrong things we do—if we don't get rid of them as soon as we notice them, they grow and grow some more, until they take over our lives and spoil everything.

I'm sure you've heard grown-ups talk about the "robe of Christ's righteousness," haven't you? That's parable talk for what happens to us when we ask Jesus to come into our hearts and make us holy like Him. It's like He puts brand-new, beautiful clothes over our old, dirty, "rat-chewed" underwear. Once we have His new robe on, He helps us get rid of the "filthy rags" we're wearing underneath.

Now, I've been told that overcoming bad habits is much easier when you're young, but being a grandma and all, I don't think that's true. It was hard when I was a kid, and it's just as hard now—as it has been all through my life. The truth is that it is *always* hard to give up wrong and choose right, but once you see the glistening robe of Jesus, you'll want one just like His!

He's got one in His closet made just especially—and only—for you. And He's really eager to see how you look in it. Then Jesus will work on getting rid of the ugly habits you might have underneath. Jesus makes it *so* much easier!

Momma and Daddy both worked at keepin' the varmints out. And they showed me that the best way to deal with sin is right away and decisively!

With a big hug,
Grandma

Chapter 24

Overnight Raisins

David came home from school one day, tossed his books on the kitchen table, and collapsed into a chair. He looked puzzled as Momma set a glass of cold milk and a couple of cookies in front of him.

"What's wrong, Dave?" Momma asked.

"Miss Millard said raisins are really just dried up grapes! Is that true?" he demanded. "She said if we put grapes on a board outside in the sunshine, pretty soon they would be raisins!"

"That's right," Momma replied.

"Hmmm," was all Dave said as he took his cookies and shuffled out the door, deep in thought.

I pondered on the mystery of grapes turning into raisins for a few minutes and then turned to help Momma finish putting the last coat of paint on the woodwork in the living room.

Every day the little house was coming closer to being finished, and I was beginning to wonder what we would ever do all day when the house was finished! Daddy worked on it every evening, and Momma did what she could in between her other chores. Then one day she declared it was ready for entertaining company and promptly invited all the church ladies to our house for a baby shower the next week!

A shower for a baby?

Now, I didn't know exactly what a baby shower was, but I could tell it was exciting and fun. And I could be there! Momma explained that it was a party for a woman who was going to have a baby soon and said it was called a shower because the new momma and baby would be showered with gifts. Everybody would dress up, play games, and have dessert.

As we worked, Momma said we'd have to go into the town of John Day the next morning to buy things to make a new dress for me to wear to the party! I just loved new dresses, so I could hardly wait to go shopping at the fabric store. Then Momma surprised me.

"No, we are shopping only at the dime store this time," she said, "because we're going to make your dress out of crepe paper."

"But I thought only streamers were made out of crepe paper," I objected. I couldn't imagine a paper dress.

"Just wait and see," was all Momma would say as I peppered her with questions.

The only thing I could picture in my head was the clothes my paper doll wore. Would my party dress be flat and with tabs on the shoulders to keep it on? What would I wear on my backside? Surely Momma wouldn't make me go to a party with a dress that covered only my front!

The raisin trick

When Daddy came home after work, he didn't even get in the door before Dave grabbed his hand and asked him about the raisins. It seems Dave had been thinking about it all afternoon and had decided to put this notion of one thing changing into another to the test.

Daddy said he could use the sawhorses to hold some boards and yes, Dave could put the grapes out to dry on those. They carefully arranged the wide boards on the south side of the house where the grapes would get the most direct sun and dry quickly.

Momma looked at Daddy with a question in her eyes as she gave Dave a cluster of grapes from the Frigidaire. Then Daddy and Dave disappeared outside again. They laid the grapes carefully one by one on the makeshift drying rack. Then they went to work on another project somewhere.

Momma kept up the quizzical looks at Daddy, but he paid no attention to her and just kept doing his work on the house.

For his part, David would work a few minutes and then dash off to see whether the grapes had turned into raisins yet. Daddy told him it would take a long time, but a long time to Daddy was much different from a long time to Dave! By bedtime he must have checked on his grapes a dozen times, and still he couldn't tell the least difference. He began to doubt that the grown-ups were telling the truth after all!

Now we didn't know it at the time, but after we'd all been in bed for a good long while Daddy tiptoed quietly to the cupboard. As he and Momma crept outside, he had a mischievous grin curling up at the corners of his mouth and a raisin box in hand! Removing all the grapes from the board, he replaced them with raisins and then sat on the top step grinning at Momma as he ate the grapes, one by one. Then they got up together and went to bed—Daddy still grinning and Momma still shaking her head.

Early the next morning Dave raced outside to check on his experiment. Then we heard a loud whoop! "Hey look, everybody!" he yelled excitedly. "I made raisins! It *worked*! I really made raisins!"

I rubbed the sleep from my eyes and stared down at his open hand thrust in front of my face. Sure enough, those were raisins all right. I was impressed with the wisdom of my big brother and the vast storehouse of knowledge he was gaining by going to school! Would I ever get to go too? After all, I needed to know this stuff just as much as he did!

"I'm going to take these to school and show the teacher!" he exclaimed.

Now it was Momma who was grinning, and Daddy who was shaking his head! Miss Millard would never believe Dave had made raisins overnight, and Daddy thought it best if he left a little early for work and stopped by the schoolhouse to do a little explaining to Dave's teacher!

When we were much older and able to handle the truth about the raisin "incident," Daddy confessed everything—and we all got a good laugh out of it! I don't know whether Daddy learned anything from all this, but for me, well, that was the fun of living with him, because you just never knew what kind of interesting mischief was brewing in his head!

Here's a little poem I really like, and I hope you'll enjoy it too.

The Summer Children

by Edgar A. Guest

I like 'em in the winter when their cheeks are slightly pale;
I like 'em in the springtime when the March wind blows a gale.
But when summer suns have tanned 'em and they're racing to and fro,
I somehow think the children make the finest sort of show.

When they're brown as little berries and they're bare of foot and head,
And they're on the go each minute where the velvet lawns are spread,
Then their health is at its finest and they never stop to rest,
Oh, it's then I think the children look and are their very best!

We've got to know the winter, and we've got to know the spring;
But for children, could I do it, unto summer I would cling.
For I'm happiest when I see 'em as a wild and merry band
Of healthy, robust youngsters that the summer sun has tanned.

Chapter 25

The Crepe-Paper Dress

After Dave was out the door and on his way to school, Momma started the car and took Mike to spend the morning with Aunt Lily and our cousin Dickie. They lived right on the way to John Day, and Mike would have a good time playing with our little cousin, because they were close to the same age.

I liked going to town with Momma when it was just the two of us. We didn't have to hurry so much, and she seemed more relaxed than when there were more kids for her to keep track of.

Sunshine mountain

The trip to John Day would take about a half hour. I knew the road well. We turned right at the corner by Shorty's gas station and headed out on the main road, enjoying the bright sunny day. The windows were rolled down, and we could hear the meadowlarks singing on the fence posts and smell the wildflowers that grew in the ditches.

There was a particular hill beside the road about five miles out of Dayville that looked to me like it surely must be the "sunshine mountain" we sang about in Sabbath School. It was right next to the road and was covered all over with sunflowers from top to bottom. It didn't have any trees or sagebrush on it—nothing but beautiful, nodding sunflowers and so many bees buzzing around you could almost smell the honey in the wind.

Little Cabin by the River

Momma and I sang the song as we drove past.

Climb, climb up Sunshine Mountain, heavenly breezes blow,
Climb, climb up Sunshine Mountain, faces all aglow.
Turn, turn from sin and doubting, looking to the sky.
Climb, climb up Sunshine Mountain, you and I!

Then we looked at each other and laughed out loud—and sang it all over again! As we got closer to town, Momma started telling me of all the different things she would need for the baby shower the next week. I didn't understand half of what she told me, but I felt very grown up and terribly important to be included in her party plans. She said we'd need two colors of crepe paper—yellow and pink because those were the colors of all the decorations. She said we'd need two packages of each color. One package would be for the "helper" dress and two others would be used to make streamers for our living room. One of my friends from Sabbath School was going to help, too, so the last package would be for her dress. Momma said I had to let her choose first whether she wanted a pink dress or a yellow one, but I sure hoped she'd pick yellow!

The dime store

Momma found a parking spot close to the dime store—that's what we might call a variety store or perhaps a dollar store of today. It had lots of small items for sale, and none of them cost more than ten cents! They sold bobby pins, clothespins, and safety pins. Evening in Paris perfume, or mothballs for your winter clothes. Even hair permanents and candy by the pound. And they definitely sold some things I'd never seen before!

Momma got a cart to put our things into, and I pushed it carefully up and down the aisles. She bought the crepe paper first, and oh, it was so pretty and crinkly! Then she went to the toy section and counted out twelve tiny pink rubber baby dolls for the party favor cups. Next, she found a big paper umbrella for the centerpiece and a greeting card for the new baby, and then she counted out twelve waxed flannel diapers held together with a small gold pin in front to use for holding the mints she had ordered at the candy counter.

"Is that everything?" she asked me. I didn't remember, so I just looked at her while she went over her list to be sure she hadn't forgotten anything. When she seemed satisfied, we moved to the counter and Momma carefully counted out the amount the clerk asked for. She counted it twice to be sure—we couldn't afford to waste money. But this was a rare and special extravagance of hospitality that she'd looked forward to sharing with her friends. Everything we bought came out to just a little over a dollar and a half. Momma said that it was less than she feared it might be. That made us both glad as we returned home and unpacked our treasures.

Sewing paper dresses

As soon as lunch was over and Mike was down for his nap, my friend Susan and her mother came over to see what we'd bought. I held my breath when Momma asked Susan whether she wanted a yellow or pink dress. I even crossed my fingers behind my back, trying to will her to choose yellow. But alas, she chose pink! I couldn't blame her, but the yellow was pretty, too, I reasoned. After all, I still got to "hostess" at the party and got the same party stuff as everyone else!

Momma got out some old dress patterns she'd made for me before. Then she and Susan's mother picked one to make our party dresses from. They were just alike except for the color. We were both very excited to have special dresses for just this one evening.

As soon as they left, Momma got out her big scissors with the black handles and pinned the pattern on the yellow crepe paper. She cut carefully on the lines then threaded the sewing machine with yellow thread.

"Are you going to *sew* the paper dress?" I asked.

"Of course I am," Momma replied. "How did you think I was going to hold it together?"

"I thought you would paste the pieces together. We always use paste on paper."

"Not this time, dear," Momma explained. "I'll make it the same way I make all your other dresses."

That was very good news to me. I was no longer afraid of having to wear a one-sided dress that was held in place with paper tabs on my shoulders. I watched in amazement while Momma's sewing machine needle flashed up and down through the paper as if it were fabric. It was going to be just like a regular dress—except that I could throw it away when it got dirty. It was kind of plain on the top, with rows of ruffles on the skirt, which Momma ruffled even more by pulling on the edges of the paper. She ruffled the edges of my short sleeves, too, and it turned out to be a beautiful dress I could hardly wait to wear!

Girls only

The days crawled by until the party date arrived. I helped Momma all afternoon by cleaning the house, making a pretty Jell-O mold, and decorating the living room for all our guests. They wouldn't come until after supper, and as soon as they did, Momma would send all the boys in our house down the road to Uncle Carl's house while the women had the shower party. Momma said this was a "girls only" occasion. (It sure was fun to be a girl!)

Just before the guests arrived, Momma helped me into my crepe-paper dress and put a matching yellow bow in my hair. Then she helped me stand on the bench in front of her dresser so I could see myself in the mirror.

Oh! I look very beautiful, I thought, *and the yellow dress is just perfect!*

Just then Susan and her mother arrived—and she looked beautiful too! We danced around the room and turned pirouettes on our toes, all the while looking at our reflection in the living room windows. This was so exciting!

Momma had made a big flat cake with yellow and pink roses on it, and now she carried it carefully from the pantry to its place of honor on the party table. Susan and I brought the paper napkins and placed them just so beside the paper cups for punch.

When everything was ready, the guests began to arrive, several to a car. With every new lady in the room, the conversation grew louder until the room was filled with happy chatter and laughter.

My friend and I passed out little pencils and slips of paper to each woman for the games they played. Then, after the new momma had opened all the gifts for her baby, we served the guests cake and punch. The lights were bright that evening, and Susan and I felt very grown up, flitting around, trying to be helpful and gracious.

The only sad thing about the party was that it ended far too soon. But the whole thing had been a huge success. After everyone had gone, Momma sank into the armchair with a happy little sigh.

"What did you think?" she asked me as I leaped past her like a ballerina.

"That was fun!" I exclaimed. "But this dress is scratchy! May I take it off now?"

Chapter 26

A Different Point of View

It seemed exciting and strange at the same time! Momma waved good-bye to Daddy and me, and I could see Dave holding Mike on his lap in the front seat as the little tan coupe rolled backward down the driveway, backed onto the highway, and sped away. That left just the two of us standing between the house and the garage with a big empty day stretching out ahead of us.

How odd for Daddy to stay home during the day and for Momma to be leaving! In fact, I couldn't remember him ever doing that before. But there was no work at the mill that day, and Momma was needed to help the big kids at school with a special project.

Ingathering fun

We don't go Ingathering anymore, but back in the olden days we did it for one week every fall, right after school opened—and every kid loved it.

Here is how it worked: about mid-September the teacher would get out a big county map and let all the students cluster around her desk while she divided the territory into smaller districts with her red pencil. Then she'd get out a ledger book and record our names, two to a line. That made one pair, and there were at least two pairs to a team and sometimes three. It was more fun to be in a group with three pairs to a car because we were more crowded that way and "the more the merrier!"

Then our teacher would assign each group to one of the volunteer drivers. Each group would huddle in a corner while other groups huddled in other places around the room. Each driver was given a boxful of leaflets that we would be giving to the people we met, and each pair of kids got a little oval metal canister with a slit in its top to hold the money we'd collect. A quick prayer for safety and blessing would be followed by a flurry of activity as each group separated to find their assigned car and driver.

We'd lug the box of leaflets along with our sack lunches and offering containers and follow our leader out to his or her car and put everything in the trunk. Then we'd all pile in, and with one kid assigned to read the map, we'd find our territory and get to work.

The point of this activity was to solicit money to help our church take care of the widows and orphans who couldn't afford food or clothing. At the same time it was an opportunity to tell people about our mission work, both in the United States and in other countries. (We each had a little memorized speech to give at the door, or sometimes right on the streets downtown.)

But for now, all this adventure lay ahead of me because I wasn't anywhere near six years old yet, and I was still too young to go.

Never mind, I thought. *Today I get to be with Daddy for the whole day!* I looked up at him in the bright sunshine, and he looked down at me, both of us trying to figure out how the day would go.

Up on the roof

"I'll tell you what," he said at last. "I'll do the hammering. When I need something from the ground, you can find it and hand it up to me from the bottom step of the ladder."

I was disappointed, but it was a start. I really wanted to be right up where he was—and hammering too! But he was worried I'd fall off the ladder or slide down the roof and hit the ground. So Daddy gathered up his tools and a bag of nails. As he started to climb the ladder, he called down over his shoulder, "You play right here where I can keep an eye on you, OK?"

He didn't need to say that, because there was no place I'd rather be! I wondered how I could climb the ladder, but I'd just have to be patient and bide my time until the opportunity showed itself.

For a while I chased the big grasshoppers that flew everywhere this time of year. They made a clicking, whirring sound as they flew, and their wings were yellow with grayish stripes. Most of them were bigger than my biggest finger now, and their feet had little barbs on them that clung tightly to my skin when I caught one. Their two big eyes were full of little eyes, and they'd turn to look at me as I held one on my finger.

I wonder what I look like to them? I thought. *Do they see as many of me as they have eyes?*

The grasshopper spit out a huge wad of "tobacco" juice that stained my finger, and I figured he couldn't be long for this world. So I let him go to enjoy his last few moments of life before he died a horrible death from lung cancer.

The Dorcas box

Next, I turned my attention to a box of old clothes and shoes stored just inside the garage. They were mostly Momma's things, and she intended to give them away to the Dorcas Society. The Dorcas ladies would sort the clothes, shoes, and other things to give away to the needy.

Right on top sat a pair of high-heeled shoes. They were white with brown on the toes and heels, and where the colors came together, there was a row of dots. When I looked more closely, I realized they were actually holes punched in the brown leather that let the white surface underneath show through. It was all quite ingenious and made such a pretty pattern. I slipped them on and looked at my feet. The shoes were awfully big on me.

Next I found a Sabbath dress Momma didn't wear anymore and pulled it over my head. It dragged on the ground, and I had to yank on the neckline to get it to stay on my shoulders, but I felt very fashionable now!

If only I had a hat, I thought as I rummaged through the box.

At last one came into view as I scattered clothes over the dirt floor. It was kind of smallish and had a short veil on the front and a bunch of fake cherries hanging on one side. I could see why Momma was giving it away!

Plopping it on my head anyway, I struggled out the door to show my finery to Daddy. The long, trailing dress made it almost impossible to walk, and the high heels finished the job! But I hobbled along as best I could until Daddy could see me.

"Look!" I cried. "Look at me!"

Daddy looked and laughed at what he saw.

"You better not let your momma see you that way!" he said, shaking his head like he always did when he was perplexed or amused.

"Go put it all back, and then I could use your help for a minute."

Wow—those were welcome words! He was going to let me help, so I changed as fast as I could and reappeared at the bottom of the ladder.

A different view—and cookies too!

"I'm out of roofing tacks," Daddy said. "Here, take this bag and fill it up again for me, will you?"

He tossed the little paper bag to the ground and pointed to the big bag from the hardware store. I scooped up handfuls of the short, stubby tacks, dashed back to the foot of the ladder, and stood as tall as I could on the bottom step, just like he told me to do.

Daddy reached down with his long arms as far as he could reach but there was still a big gap between my hands and his. Reluctantly, he descended the ladder to retrieve the tacks before climbing up to the rooftop again.

"You did a good job!" he commended. "Next time you can climb up to meet me."

My heart skipped a beat. Now I wished I hadn't filled the bag so full of tacks! This day was getting better already.

I played some more, hoping that Daddy would need something soon. And sure enough, after a little while, he asked if I would bring him a glass of cool water from the house. He said to use one of Momma's plastic glasses so we wouldn't break it.

Dashing into the house and pulling a chair over to the cupboard, I climbed high enough to reach the handle, got a tall plastic glass off the shelf, and filled it with cool water. I walked carefully so I wouldn't spill any of it on the ground on the way back, but I stopped suddenly at the bottom of the ladder. How was I going to climb up with the water in one hand?

I put my foot on the bottom rung and stepped up. *That wasn't so hard! I'll just have to climb differently, that's all.* Instead of putting only one foot on each rung, I'd just have to put both feet on each rung.

Little Cabin by the River

Daddy looked down, coaching me at every step until I reached the top. How different everything looked from up here! I could see so much farther in every direction—it felt like I was in a whole new world!

"Can I stay up here for a little while, Daddy?"

Daddy said I could, and then helped me turn around so I could sit on the ladder's top rung. My tummy felt funny and fluttery as the warm soft breeze ruffled my hair. Meadowlarks sang in the fields, and little fluffy white clouds sailed smoothly in the sky overhead. Sights and sounds were clearer up here, and it seemed much more peaceful than being on the ground. What a wonderful, beautiful day it was. I filled my lungs with its fresh warmth as I sighed in contentment.

I told Daddy I wanted to live on the garage roof, but he said for me to go down again. So I climbed down to the ground, but my heart was still up there where the birds flew and I felt free.

The day was perfect now that I had been allowed up where Daddy worked, but it was about to get even better!

The sun was getting hotter now, so Daddy took off his shirt to keep working. Every little while he'd pull out his big cloth handkerchief and wipe his brow while scanning to see how many more shingles the roof needed.

My stomach growled, and I began to wonder how much longer until lunch. Daddy must have been thinking the same thing, because pretty soon he straightened up and said, "I could use a couple of cookies about now. How about you?"

Cookies? Oh, yeah! I could always use a couple of cookies!

He told me where Momma hid them in the pantry and asked me to bring the whole package to him. I returned in a flash, climbing the ladder in the same way I had before. As I reached the top, Daddy was sitting on the roof ridge.

"Come on up!" he said. "Just climb on all fours and go slow. You'll be fine."

How could one day hold so much fun and adventure? I wondered. How did I get so lucky as to be spending the whole day with Daddy—and without anyone else around?

I had him all to myself, and he was letting me help him, and he was allowing me to be with him up on the roof. All this, and cookies besides!

I hung the bag of cookies from my mouth as I crawled with both hands and feet up the slope to the crest of the roof. The higher I went, the more glorious everything was! I straddled the ridge just like Daddy as we sat on the very top and ate sugar cookies with big grains of sugar sprinkled on the top of each crinkly treat.

We sat and looked out for a long time. Daddy pointed out buildings I couldn't see from the ground, and I cried out in delight as the bluebirds and swallows swooped around our heads. It was a golden time for my daddy and me. We didn't want it to end, and he procrastinated as long as he could before returning to the nails and shingles.

He only had few more to go, so he finished quickly before he got a sunburn. Then we went inside to eat the sandwiches Momma had left us.

Not much later Momma pulled up with the boys, and my time with Daddy was over. David was excited about his adventures with Ingathering, and little Mike was ready for a nap.

Everyone had enjoyed a good day—but no one had a better day than I had!

Heart to heart

As I've grown older I've thought about that day with my father and how it's a lot like spending time with my *other* Father.

If you're old enough to have forgotten what it's like to be a toddler, you should get down on your hands and knees and see the world from that perspective for a while. Then stand up and notice how things seem to move into a different position—and again if you get up on a ladder.

It's like that with God too. When we first start out, we see things from a knee-high level, and we can't understand why God does some of the things He does (or why He asks us to do certain things and not do others).

However, if we keep spending time with Him, we'll grow taller and see things differently. When He knows the time is right, He'll invite us to start climbing higher. And with every upward step, we'll see farther and find ourselves understanding His view more and more!

When I lost my doll Cynthia, I was really truly only knee-high and hardly more than a toddler. No wonder I couldn't understand why God didn't save her from the wolves when I asked Him to! But with age and experience came a change of perspective, and I learned not to worry about that seemingly unanswered prayer any more. I know there was a good reason; I just don't know what it was—yet! I still can't explain why it happened as it did, but that doesn't matter. What *does* matter is that every single time I've trusted God, I've inched a step higher in my understanding. It's brought me closer to seeing things the way He does!

Come up on the roof. The view is grand!
Grandma

Chapter 27

Ante, Ante, Over?

Merriment and mayhem filled the house and the yard. What pure joy—the cousins were here!

They came piling in just after lunch on a sunny Sunday afternoon, changing the tone of the day from routine to rowdy and rambunctious. When we all got together, it seemed as if there were fifteen exciting things going on at once. Sometimes it just put me into a real dither about which group to join.

Because I was inside when the aunties, uncles, and younger cousins trooped in, at first I listened to the grown-ups talk and laugh while I played with Kathy, Dickie, Mike, and Duane. You can hear the most interesting conversations when grown-ups think you're not listening! I liked the mysterious feeling of power that came from having a secret and keeping it to myself.

Catching an eyeful

Pretty soon, the boys went their way, and Kathy and I went to my room to play "girl stuff." It wasn't long before we'd pulled out all the dolls I owned from under the bed, dressed them, fed them, and put them down for their naps. Then we dressed up in some of Momma's old housedresses and put the dolls in the buggy for a walk all around the living room and up and down the hallway. But after a while I noticed that my older cousins hadn't come in. Suddenly, my dolls lost all their charm, and an alarming thought raced through my mind—*They're outside having fun without me!* The horror of that idea stopped me dead in my tracks. Turning around quickly, I dashed out the kitchen door in a dead run. Poor Kathy. She just stood there in the middle of the hall, her mouth hanging open, wondering what had gotten into me!

Little dust clouds swirled around my feet as I sped across the driveway, scanning the yard in every direction as I tried to determine where the big kids were. They weren't too hard to find, of course, because of all the racket they made. *Oh! They're having such a great time, and I'm missing out!*

Now I need to let you in on a little secret about the "older" cousins and my big brother Dave. They were older than I was, but sometimes they just weren't *that* much smarter! Keep in mind that I was barely five when this happened, and they were just six to eight years of age, so obviously, none of us had the good judgment that comes from time and experience!

All that filled my mind at that moment was to get in on the fun as fast as I could. I could hear laughter and shouts coming from behind the garage, and I careened wildly around the corner, just in time to hear Gary yell from the other side, "Ante, ante, over!"

There stood Sharon and David, looking expectantly toward the garage roof, waiting for the ball to appear.

Ante, ante, over is an old-fashioned game from long ago made just for kids who didn't have a lot of stuff with which to play. All it takes is a rubber ball, or maybe a soft ball, and a shed or garage for a barrier, so you can't see what the other team is doing. You *can* play this game with only two people, if that's all you have, but it's lots more fun if you have at least four or more players.

You pick two teams and put them on opposite sides of the building. Originally, the whole name was ante, ante, over the shanty, but we just said the first part when we played. Anyway, the idea is to throw the ball over the shed, hoping the other team doesn't catch it. It has to fly over the roof or it doesn't count. But you can throw it from any angle to try to catch the other team off guard. If they *do* snag it before it hits the ground, the one who caught it runs around the building and tries to tag somebody. Then the one who is tagged is taken prisoner and has to play for the other team. If nobody catches it, the ones who missed simply throw it back over the shed or garage or whatever, calling out the warning, "Ante, ante, over!" and the game goes on.

From the far side, Ron sang out, "Pig's tail!" which meant the ball didn't quite make it over the top of the roof. That was good news to me because now I could get close enough to take part in the action!

"Ante, ante, over!" Gary called again. At the very same moment a beautiful red croquet ball sailed into view! Somehow, in all the excitement, it never dawned on me anyone would be playing ante, ante, over with a croquet ball! Who'd have ever thought?

The sun was partly in my eyes, but I dashed toward the spot where I thought the ball would land—my arms stretched wide, hoping I'd catch it before Dave or Sharon did.

Well, I was successful beyond my wildest dreams, all right. I caught that shiny red wooden ball directly—with my left eye socket.

The impact knocked me to the ground, and I couldn't see anything for a few minutes as blood filled my eye and ran like tears down my face.

"Why did you go and do that?" David asked, obviously annoyed. "Don't you know you're supposed to catch with your hands?"

Sharon was more sympathetic as she slipped her arms under me to help me stand. By this time Gary and Ron had run around the corner to see what all the ruckus was about. When they saw me, they just stared and didn't say anything, but they looked scared.

My eye was swelling fast and turning purple at an alarming rate. "I want to find Momma," was all I could say, so Sharon led me carefully back inside where all the grown-ups were still laughing and talking.

Suddenly, they all stopped talking. They all stared at me, and they kept right on staring until I heard Momma wail, "What happened to her?"

Sharon started to explain, but the boys broke in.

"She ruined our game. She shouldn't have even been out there!" they shouted. "She doesn't know how to play ante, ante, over—she ran right under the ball and let it hit her in the eye! It's all her own fault!"

Momma had rushed to my side to get a better look at the damage, which by now was quite shocking. My eye was swollen entirely shut and was beginning to turn awful shades of red, green, and purple—the colors all running together. And now it was as big as a tennis ball!

"A rubber ball wouldn't do that kind of damage," Daddy observed. "What were you guys throwing around out there?"

Momma bathed my eye with cool water, as Dave spoke up innocently, "I couldn't find the one we always use, so we used a croquet ball instead."

At this statement, all the aunties and uncles gasped with dismay as Momma scooped me up and hurried me to the car.

Daddy kept asking, "What were you guys thinking?"

Strong medicine

Daddy drove while I cuddled close to Momma. She kept a cold cloth on my aching head, but I felt dizzy and sick as we sped the thirty miles to the hospital. Momma kept trying to soothe my throbbing head by stroking and kissing it. It helped a lot, but what she didn't know was that my heart hurt too. I wanted so much to be included with all the kids, but it seemed the older ones didn't really want me around much of the time. By trying to be a part of their fun, I'd only earned their scorn.

Anyway, when we got to the emergency room, the nurses took one look at my disfigured face and placed me right onto the X-ray table. People came from all over the hospital, poking their heads in through the door to look at my swollen eye. By now, it had grown to the size of a grapefruit! They'd shake their heads in disbelief and make little clicking sounds with their tongues. Or they'd ask Momma to tell them how it happened—and then shake their heads even more!

Finally the doctor came in. He said that he couldn't see any fractures and that he thought I'd heal just fine. "But," he added, "I can't be sure about her vision until the swelling goes down a bit."

Momma's mouth made a tight little line, and she nodded to show she understood. Daddy just turned his hat around in his hands and said nothing. On the other hand, I was ready to get out of this place where everybody stared at me.

Soon we were on our way back home, much to my relief. Those curious people dressed in white made me nervous. I kept wondering what they might do to me! There were so many of them, and they were all bigger than me. Who knew what tortures they could think up if they put their minds to it. Oh, blessed escape!

The breeze coming through the open windows felt cool and good on my fevered face as the ache began to ease a little and the knot in my stomach started to loosen. We didn't talk much on the way home, but it sure felt good to be going toward home instead of toward the hospital!

As we rounded the last curve, we could see Shorty's gas station ahead, and Daddy said we'd better stop.

"Fill 'er up," Daddy called out as Shorty ambled toward our car.

"How ya doin', Everett?" he asked as he put the nozzle into the tank and began washing our windshield.

"We're doing all right," Daddy answered.

Shorty lifted the hood and checked the motor oil and water levels and then let it slam down with a huge *bang*! The hood always sounded like that when it dropped into place, but today it startled me, and I sat bolt upright.

"Ah! You've got one of the young'uns with you today!" He sounded jovial as he rested his elbows on the car window and his chin in his hands. "Well, young lady, looks like you tangled with a wild cat!" winking at Momma as he said it. He peered at my face from every angle, just like the doctors and nurses had, but Shorty didn't scare me at all. His heart was pure gold, and it shone out of his twinkling eyes.

"This calls for strong medicine," he muttered as he shuffled toward the tiny building that served as both garage and office.

I knew what that meant! Candy!

He returned with a whole fistful of penny candy and shoved it through the open window as I held both hands open as wide as I could stretch them.

"There!" he said with determination. "You eat every bit of it yourself. Just one piece a day until you get well. If you run out, just come on back for more." What a dear old man he was! His "medicine" did a whole lot to take away the sting of the rejection I had felt earlier.

Every day I felt better and better until I even forgot my eye was still swollen and bruised. But when Momma would take me to the store with her, or we would go to Sabbath School and church, everybody would gather around and bend over me—staring. That's when I'd remember I still hadn't fully healed.

Eventually the swelling went down, the bruises faded, and I could see just fine. God surely was taking care of me through all those wild misadventures, harrowing turns of events, and dangerous daring-dos. I'll leave it to you to figure out the many morals of this story, but I do have one request: please don't heave croquet balls over the garage roof—or anywhere else, for that matter!

Chapter 28

Up in Smoke

From far away there came the sound of wailing, and it roused me from a deep sleep. But my bed felt so good and cozy that I didn't want to wake up. I just rolled over and tried to doze some more.

But the wailing continued to rise and fall, and it was getting louder. We rarely heard sirens way out in Dayville. Once in a while the sheriff would pull over somebody for speeding, but we didn't have a police station, and the nearest fire truck was in John Day. So this commotion seemed highly irregular!

I wondered what was happening, but I was just too sleepy to care, so when the fire engine eventually zoomed past our house and things quieted down again, I went back to sleep.

All gone!

Early the next morning Uncle Bill woke us up by pounding on the kitchen door and shouting, "Everett! Get up! There's been a fire!"

He sounded very excited and kept on pounding until Daddy answered the door in his pajamas.

Uncle Bill's hair was all mussed up, his clothes smelled smoky, and he was covered with soot as he stamped his feet on the rug. "The mill's gone!" was all he said as he plopped into the nearest chair.

He hung his head and repeated, "It's all gone! Nothing left—burned to the ground—the mill's just—*gone.*"

He told us how he awoke to the reflection of fire on his bedroom walls as the light of the flames came in through his window. He had rushed off to help put out the fire, only to discover that the burning building was the mill.

It was too late to save it from the fire, and by the time the fire truck had arrived from John Day, the roof had fallen in and the walls were collapsing. The men had used the few water hoses they could find, but it was just not enough to put out the raging flames.

Daddy hurriedly threw on his old clothes and jumped into Uncle Bill's pickup to go see the damage for himself. The rest of us just looked at each other in shock and wondered whether it was really true! *Where will Daddy work if the mill is gone? What will happen to us?* I wondered.

No job

After a long time Daddy came home and said it really was true. There had been a fire in the night that burned the lumber mill to the ground, and now it was just a smoldering heap of ashes and twisted metal. Nobody could work there anymore—and that meant that Daddy and all of our uncles didn't have jobs anymore.

Momma looked at Daddy with disbelief. They had struggled so hard to make a start in this wild, windy place out next to nowhere. Things had just begun to look like they might get better—and now *this.*

However, after a few hours, determination took the place of discouragement, and Momma started talking about what to do next. Daddy found out there was a logging company across the state that would hire some of the men who had lost their jobs to the fire, so he set out with Uncle Bill and Uncle Carl to sign on. They took one car and left all their families at home while they checked things out. If they got hired, they would find places to live in the new town before they'd come back to get us.

When they returned, they seemed excited about finding jobs and houses for all of us. Daddy tried to convince Uncle Don and Aunt Lily to join our moving caravan, but they decided to return to Pendleton, Oregon, and work at the mill there instead.

I felt sad that they wouldn't be coming with us. It seemed that our extended family was breaking apart. They promised to visit as soon as they could, though, and Aunt Lily said she'd write letters to keep in touch, so I felt better.

Adventures await

Daddy sold the little house he'd built with his very own hands, and Momma packed everything into boxes. Then one day, Daddy came home pulling a trailer along behind the little coupe, and we all loaded it with our belongings.

The next morning we'd be off to another adventure in a place I'd never seen before. I tried to imagine what it was like from the stories Daddy had told. He said there were lots of tall trees—whole forests of them—and new wildflowers to see. He said it was greener because it rained more; that fact thrilled Momma to the core! But the best thing of all was this: Sutherlin, Oregon, was much closer to the ocean, and Daddy would take us there as soon as he could.

My heart sang with excitement at what the future held, and I was eager to forge ahead. But as we left Dayville, a lump arose in my throat as I pressed my nose against the glass of the rear window. I watched our little house growing smaller and smaller as we drove away. It looked sad, standing empty and alone beside the road, and I thought it must be wondering why we were leaving it behind.

On our way out of town, we passed the other houses we'd lived in: the house where I accidentally drove the tractor; Miner's Mansion, where so many good times rolled; and last, the little cabin near the river on one side of the highway, the little white church/one-room schoolhouse on the other. In my mind, they all gathered together into a little cluster that meant "home" as they faded from view.

At last the highway made a curve, and we started to climb into the mountains. I whirled around to look forward and see where we were going next. I stood up to look between the front seats so I could see the road ahead.

Who knows what's around the next corner or over the next rise?

Ah, the sweet, tantalizing aroma of the unknown—of adventures yet to be lived. They beckoned me onward!

Epilogue

After the Dust Has Settled

Well, many years have come and gone since these delightful escapades filled my life with joyful adventures, expanding horizons, and developing relationships. All that remains are some old, faded photographs and a world of wonderful memories. And, of course, the little girl who lived them still exists deep in my heart.

Now if you're still just a kid, hooray for you! You're right in the middle of your "good ol' days." The very things, people, and events that fill your life with excitement, adventure, and imagination today are the stuff of your fondest memories tomorrow. Cherish every minute you spend with your family, learn all you can about God, investigate every corner of His creation, and be as helpful as you possibly can be to your parents and teachers.

Dear grandchild, open your eyes wide to the whole wonderful world of discovery and fling open all the doors and windows of your heart for Jesus to live there. That way, you'll have the best childhood possible!

* * * * *

But now I want to talk to the grown-ups for a little bit.

After some of the dust from the uproar of my early years settled, time rolled by, life happened, and I sort of lost that little girl inside. Marriage, children, jobs, heartache, tears, and tragedies—all of that came to my door, until one day I was almost startled to realize how far I had drifted from my beginnings.

Makes me wonder about *you.* Where are *you* these days? Have you kind of lost the person you once were? The good news is, it's not too late to return to those values!

Think back to how you felt in your *own* "good ol' days." The warmth and comfort of family, the security of learning about Jesus' love for you, the sense of belonging that came from worshiping together every week, and the blessings of family worship every night.

Is there an ache in your heart from missing all these? Why don't you just turn right around and come on home? It's suppertime, and there's a light in the window to guide your way. Inside, the whole family longs for and anticipates your return. And we will receive you with open arms and great joy! We have missed you so. Please come back.

* * * * *

Or maybe your early years weren't filled with happy memories of family, church, and faith in God. Maybe you remember only pain, loneliness, and abuse. The good news is, it's not too late!

Jesus will give you a whole new infancy and childhood filled with all the things you missed the first time around! Have you ever wondered what all those "Christians" are talking about when they speak of the "new birth" experience?

Well, here it is—people are always saying, "You can't choose your parents." But that's only true in the biological sense. You *can* choose to have a new Father, a perfectly wonderful Big Brother, and a multitude of loving new brothers and sisters, aunts, uncles, and cousins! We want you in our family. We're not perfect, of course, but we'll travel the road together!

And isn't that what you really want anyway? Togetherness?

With God as your Father on the one hand, Jesus as your protective Big Brother on the other hand, and the Holy Spirit hovering all around and *in* you (on the third hand!), you can be nurtured into a whole new life. You can make new, fresh memories, as God kindly, gently, and ever so lovingly re-parents you. He'll gradually erase all your pain and despair, and He'll fill you with joy, purpose, and hope.

Wherever you are, whatever you've done—or not done—please come home. It's never too late to have a wonderful childhood!

With much love,
Grandma

The Hyacinth CHRONICLES

*Meet Hyacinth Gail Pipsner,
a charming and mischievous second-grader whose antics
will leave you laughing out loud. Hyacinth is the daughter of Pastor and Mrs.
Pipsner, and the second-grader with the most active imagination is Mrs. Raju's classroom.*

The Hyacinth Chronicles
by Patty Froese Ntihemuka

Hyacinth Doesn't Go to Jail • Hyacinth loves her parents. She loves her best friend, Ruby. She *loves* to talk—she even loves her big brother, Nolan, which gets her into big trouble with the school bully.

Hyacinth Doesn't Miss Christmas • Hyacinth's curiosity nearly causes her to miss Christmas—will Nolan get all her presents?
Paperback, 160 Pages
ISBN 10: 0-8163-2372-0

The Hyacinth Chronicles 2
by Patty Froese Ntihemuka

Hyacinth Doesn't Grow Up • Hyacinth has a BIG problem: she can't decide what to be when she grows up—and no matter who she asks, no one can help her! Only Nolan has a suggestion—a bulldog! Oh dear!

Hyacinth Doesn't Drown • Hyacinth is afraid to wash her hair, let alone take swimming lessons! And maybe Nolan is right—maybe she really is too dense to float! Paperback, 160 Pages
ISBN 10: 0-8163-2386-0

PP Pacific Press®
Publishing Association
"Where the Word Is Life"

Three ways to order:

1	Local	Adventist Book Center®
2	Call	1-800-765-6955
3	Shop	AdventistBookCenter.com